BROTHERS IN ARMS

SEAL Defender

SEAL Protector

SEAL Guardian

SEAL DEFENDER

LESLIE NORTH

BLURB

Mark Aleki Rogers left the Navy SEALs behind, but he found another use for his special skills. He and his fellow "Brothers-in-Arms" now run an intense boot camp that trains civilians to survive extreme situations. Mark's size is intimidating, but the half-Samoan surfer is an eternal optimist. A suspicious string of suicides among SEALs, however, has Mark convinced it's murder. He's determined to get to the bottom of it…quietly. If he doesn't, a murderer may go free.

Reporter Geneva Rios has come to the California coast looking for a story. The recent SEAL suicides are connected to the Brothers-in-Arms, and Geneva wants to know more. The interview she's hoping for, though, comes at a price. The smoking-hot SEAL won't talk unless she completes his training course. If she can survive Mark's audition, she'll have the angle she needs. Spending more time with Mark has its own perks, but for the exotic brunette, exposing the Navy SEALs is more than just a story…it's personal.

As the heat between them reaches its boiling point, the pair puts more than their heads together. But with their own lives in danger, can they catch a killer before it's too late?

Thank you for purchasing 'SEAL Defender'
(Brothers In Arms Series Book One)

Get SIX full-length, highly-rated Leslie North Novellas FREE!
Over 548 pages of best-selling romance with a combined 634
FIVE STAR REVIEWS!

Sign-up to her mailing list and get your FREE books:

leslienorthbooks.com/sign-up-for-free-books

For all books by Leslie North visit:

Her Website: LeslieNorthBooks.com

Facebook: www.facebook.com/leslienorthbooks

TABLE OF CONTENTS

CHAPTER ONE

Mark Aleki Rogers rode out the last crests of the giant wave all the way to the shallows, murmuring quietly, *"Ola ma le alofa fua."*

Live and love freely.

Yep. That was his motto. Or, at least as freely as the events of the last few months would allow. Two funerals in six months. There was definitely something wrong.

Sure, there were guys who came back from combat so bruised and battered emotionally that they couldn't cope and killed themselves, but the two guys who had worked for him as instructors at his security firm, *Brothers In Arms*, hadn't fit that bill. Not at all.

In fact, Mark couldn't shake the strong suspicion that they weren't suicides at all.

Too many things didn't add up.

He jumped off his customized Proctor Mendia Surfboard, a gift to himself last year and one he had yet to get enough use of, and waded to the shore. Looking at his watch, he sighed.

"Leila is waiting," he reminded himself, as he looked back toward the ocean.

He'd love to stay out here the rest of the afternoon and catch more waves, for the water was the only place, he could live completely in the moment these days but his sister, Leila, was expecting him. She'd said she wanted help unloading a new shipment of ice cream for her seaside diner, but Mark knew from long experience that whenever Leila asked for his assistance, it was never that simple.

"I hope this new ice cream is good, sis. What am I saying, all ice cream is good." He chuckled at his own comment knowing that he wouldn't be heading back out to the surf anytime soon not when family needed him.

In the Samoan culture, you did anything for family. Family came first. Always. *Aiga* was the Samoan word for family and one his mother had emblazoned on his and his sister's mind from an earlier age. Now, it was part of his DNA, just another facet of who he was, which was why he didn't mind helping out in the restaurant.

His mom always blamed his inquisitive nature and high moral standards on his island heritage as well, but Mark knew better. Those skills had come directly from his time as a Navy SEAL. Honor, integrity, fortitude. If Hell Week didn't drill those into a guy, nothing would.

That was another reason he was suspicious about those deaths.

Taking one's own life was a sign of hopelessness.

And rule number one for SEALs—there was always hope.

He planned to do some nosing around into the cases later to put his own mind at ease. He'd have to do it on the down low though. No sense drawing law enforcement's attention at this point. Not until he'd gathered the information, he needed.

After one last, longing look back at the excellent surf rolling in off the California coast, Mark tucked his board beneath his arm and started to jog the half mile to his sister's place. Sure, he was still dripping wet and covered in salt and sand, Leila would most likely give him hell for it too, but hey. After serving his country faithfully as a SEAL officer for eight years and now as a busy small business owner himself, she'd have to take what she got. The afternoon sun beat down on his shaved head and made the slight shadow of dark stubble on his scalp itch. Yeah, a shower would've been good, but duty called.

Wearing a pair of neon blue men's surf shorts and nothing else, he ran down the beach. Mark couldn't help admiring the stunning beauty of the landscape. Sheer dark cliffs lined the sunbaked sand and jagged rocks jutted from the ocean waters. A colony of sea lions basked on a shoal, honking, grunting and generally causing a ruckus. The air smelled of salt, decaying seaweed and fish and if he closed his eyes, he could almost imagine himself in Samoa instead of California. Not that he'd ever visited his mother's homeland, but it was certainly on his bucket list someday.

Mark rounded another cliff, and then slowed his pace as two familiar figures approached from the other direction. What the hell? This was supposed to be his day off from the office.

CHAPTER TWO

The shaggy blond guy raised a hand in greeting. Jace Stevens, also an ex-Navy SEAL and one of Mark's business partners, was a bit younger and shorter than he was, but the man was a mechanical genius; never met an engine or piece of equipment he couldn't fix, which made him extremely handy to have around even if he was an enigma. Who the hell grew up in Wyoming yet hated horses and cows?

"Where the hell you been, man?" Jace demanded.

"Surfing," Mark called back. Like it wasn't obvious. When he wasn't working or helping his family, you could find Mark in the ocean. "What's up?"

"You look like shit, that's what's up, bro," Vann Highrider, Mark's other business partner, called out. The three of them had served in the same security unit together in the Middle East. After the military, they'd remained friends and had started Brothers In Arms to train civilians in the same tactics they'd learned from the military. Vann was half Cherokee and all attitude, looking like he walked straight off some old western movie set with his long dark hair and penetrating dark stare, though these days he could pass for just about any nationality. Another useful asset. Plus, he was also the best-damned tracker Mark had ever met. You need someone or something found, Vann was your man.

"Leila sent us to find you." Vann gave him a disapproving once-over appraisal. "She's not going to be happy."

"What? Why?" Mark slowed to a walk beside his buddies and checked his watch again. "I'm not that late. And who died and appointed you two my babysitters, huh?"

At his poor choice of words, given the recent deaths, all three cringed.

"Sorry," Mark said.

Vann muttered something under his breath Mark didn't quite catch while Jace just snorted.

"You done looking into what happened with Rick and Jon yet?" Jace asked him.

"Not yet." Mark slicked a hand over his damp scalp. "Plan to stop by the courthouse later to see copies of the death certificates. If I turn on the charm, maybe I can get that new little clerk on staff to show them to me without putting in a formal request."

"Charm, huh?" Jace asked, one brow raised.

Mark shrugged. "Figured I'd offer her a free hot fudge sundae."

"Is that what they're calling it these days?" Jace laughed.

Vann shook his head, his lips compressed. "Nice."

Together they walked up the beach to a small-whitewashed café with a deck open toward the Pacific. His sister had started Scoops Café and Ice Cream once her kids were in school to have something to keep her busy while her husband worked. That had been five years ago. Now, business was booming and her tiny diner was packed with tourists taking the scenic drive up Highway 1 to San Francisco. Today though, the tables outside were oddly empty. As he approached, Mark's suspicions grew. Yep. Something was off here. "Why did Leila call you guys? There can't be *that* much ice cream to move."

The guys exchanged a look, one Mark had seen before when they'd served together in Afghanistan. It usually meant Look Out, Danger Ahead. But they were home. They were safe. They and their business were all but worshipped in tiny Ortega, California, a little coastal town of less than two thousand citizens. Hell, Brothers In Arms Security practically kept Ortega on the map, for Christ's sake. They brought in a constant influx of travelers to the area for their classes, along with the money those same travelers spent in the area.

Frowning, Mark stowed his surfboard in the sand beside the restaurant and then climbed the wooden stairs up to the deck and tromped inside—barefoot, still wet and sand-encrusted—and squinted into the silent dark interior. Yeah. Things were *so* not right here. His military-trained instincts went on high alert. The place was always buzzing with conversation, food, and fun. But today…

"Surprise!" Leila shouted, springing up from behind the lunch counter. Soon cheers erupted around Mark as townsfolk and tourists alike clapped and shouted and smacked him on the back in congratulations. Their mom, Sefina, still pretty and spry even at sixty-five, walked out of the kitchen with a cake lit with twenty-eight candles, singing, "Happy Birthday".

"Smile," Vann growled, nudging Mark hard in the side, warning flashing in his dark eyes. "Leila went to a lot of trouble for this."

"Yeah, man." Jace grinned. "Most people are happy to have a party thrown in their honor."

Mark wanted to be happy, honest he did. But the whole damned thing just cut too close to the bone. His sister of all people knew better than to keep secrets from him. He hated secrets.

Leila walked up to them, her dark brown gaze sparkling with anger as it darted from Jace to Vann and then back again. "Jeez, you guys couldn't clean him up first?"

"Hey, you said to get him here." Vann crossed his arms, his expression flat. "Here he is."

"Seriously, this is about as clean as you're going to get him on his day off, LeLi," Jace added. "You know he's practically Aquaman during his free time."

Mark glanced around at all the happy people, all the festive streamers and decorations, but all he could think of was the last birthday surprise he'd received. He'd just turned ten and his dad had gotten him a new surfboard, top of the line and the latest design. The thing had to cost at least a month's salary all gleaming white in the sun with lines hand carved to slice the water like a scalpel and catch even the harshest waves.

Except it didn't cost his dad anything because he'd stolen it.

Surprise!

Secrets led to nothing but heartbreak. Secrets were the devil's own work. Or his dad's.

In Mark's mind, the devil and his dad were one and the same.

Without a word, Mark pushed his way through the crowd and out the front door into the parking lot, ignoring his sister's calls for him to stay and have cake. He needed to be alone, needed some air and space to clear his head. Needed to get his shit together before he faced the inevitable wrath of his family over his abrupt departure from the party inside.

"Not into the whole surprise party scene, huh?" a female voice said.

He halted in his tracks and scanned the area. There, next to a black SUV with the hood up stood a girl. A very pretty girl, Mark noted as he moved closer. He cocked his chin toward her vehicle. "Having some trouble? And how'd you know about my party?"

"No. No trouble." She slammed her hood down and wiped her hands on a rag before extending one. "I'm Geneva, by the way. Geneva Rios. I heard them yell "surprise" inside. I put two and two together. Didn't know the party was for you though."

"Nice to meet you, Geneva Rios." Mark shook her hand then perused her from head to toe. Dark red hair, tanned skin, full lips, and hazel eyes that leaned more toward green than brown. She stood a good foot shorter than his own six-foot-two height and looked maybe twenty-four, twenty-five tops. Curves in all the right places. Her smile though, wide and sweet, with just a hint of naughty, was what really drew him in. God, he loved a woman with a wicked smile.

"Yep. Today's my birthday," he said, still staring at those lips of hers.

"Really?" She raised a brow. "And here I forgot your present."

If Mark didn't know better, he'd think she was flirting. But they'd just met and he was cautious enough not to fall for every gorgeous woman in his path, no matter how tempting. Besides, for all he knew, Vann and Jace set this situation up just to keep him on the property.

Wouldn't be the first time they'd pulled some shit like that.

"Sure you don't need help?" He might be suspicious as hell, but he was still a gentleman.

"No." She stared at him a moment too long, then turned back to her car. "Just checking my oil. Why don't you like birthdays?"

"Why do you care?"

"I'm an inquisitive girl," she said. "You ex-military?"

Hackles up, Mark crossed his arms. Several reporters had descended on tiny Ortega, California after Jon's suicide, most of them looking for the next hot, salacious headline to sell their story. Mark had refused to speak to any of them. He wasn't about to start now either, regardless of how attractive said reporter might be. "Does it matter?"

Geneva pointed to one of the tattoos on his right bicep, an eagle holding a trident, with an anchor and a pistol in front. "Navy SEAL?"

He didn't answer.

"Right." Geneva winked then tossed her rag aside and placed her hands on her hips. "I probably wouldn't want to pledge my allegiance to them either after all the shitty stuff they've done."

Both offended and more intrigued than he cared to admit, Mark stepped back and shook his head. "Tell me why the hell you're really here before I evict you from the premises, Ms. Rios. If that's even your real name."

"Yes, it's my real name. Would you pick that as an alias?" She gave him a deadpan look and crossed her arms, thrusting her breasts higher beneath the scoop neck of her tank top. "I'm here to see if you'll let me interview you."

Bingo. He decided to play dumb to see how far she'd take this. "For what?"

"I'm a reporter for the National Tribune. I'm covering the recent epidemic of SEAL suicides. You know, those guys who get discharged, come home, then off themselves for no apparent reason." A flicker of dark emotion passed through her pretty hazel eyes before he could identify it. "Figured since you knew the last two victims personally, you might be able to give me some insight as to why they killed themselves."

Cursing under his breath, Mark turned away. To say he'd known the last two victims was an understatement. They were like part of his family. They'd served in Mark's SEAL unit in Kabul and his soul still ached every day that they were gone. War brought men together and created bonds stronger than almost anything else did. The last thing he wanted to do was dishonor his fallen comrades' memories by spilling his guts to some scandal rag with the worst reputation for only chasing the next big profit headline. "No interviews."

"They were your employees at one time though, right?" Geneva trailed along beside Mark as he headed back toward the diner's entrance, a small digital recorder in her hand. Going back inside wasn't ideal, but it was better than staying out here and dodging her questions. He didn't answer her.

"Don't worry," she said. "This thing is off until you give me permission."

"Which part of 'No Interviews' didn't you understand?" Mark growled, his tone razor sharp. "Leave me alone, Ms. Rios."

For the second time in one day, Mark betrayed the good manners his mom had taught him to say proper goodbyes and stalked away without another word.

CHAPTER THREE

"Just checking my oil," Geneva grumbled to herself nearly an hour later. If it were physically possible to kick one's own ass, she would've tried. What had ever possessed her to even consider rigging her distributor cap to trick an interviewee into talking to her? It went against every journalistic ethic she had and completely wasn't her style.

Her boss had casually planted the seed of the idea during their last conversation before she'd left town, claiming it wouldn't really be an interview. It would be research, but it still didn't sit right with Geneva. And yeah, maybe Mark Rogers had refused any and all interviews since his less-than-cordial run in with the press after his discharge from the Navy; maybe desperate times did call for desperate measures.

Geneva wasn't that desperate.

Nor did she plan to be either.

About thirty seconds into her boss's ill-advised scheme, she'd changed her mind and attempted to repair what damage she'd done. By then though, Mark had been behind her, and she'd had to slam the hood closed to hide the evidence of her stupidity. Only problem was, now she couldn't remember what went where and it served her right for abandoning her ethics.

Good journalists didn't need tricks to get their story.

14

The hot sun beat down on her back and she felt more parched than the barren flatlands she'd passed on her way into this godforsaken little town. The white tank top she wore stuck to her slick skin and it seemed every visible inch of her was covered in grease smears and dirt. And her hair—just a bit longer than shoulder length and always leaning toward frizzy—had ended up in a high ponytail. Forget fashion. When things got rough, as they always did for her, she was all about keeping her head down and powering through.

At least she'd dressed for comfort today for the drive here, in jean shorts, instead of her usual work attire of a crisp white button down and black pantsuit. All that fabric would've been killer.

Speaking of killing…

It was a good thing her boss at the newspaper was currently sitting about two-hundred miles to the north. Otherwise, she would've marched right into his cushy office overlooking Lombard Street and given him a sizable piece of her mind. He'd swore that undoing the wires and then reattaching them later would be easy, but the damned SUV still wouldn't start.

Seems the fake malfunction had now become a real pain in her ass.

Frustrated, she slammed the hood closed once more before glancing around the nearly empty parking lot. Most of the party guests had departed and honestly, she couldn't blame them. If she'd driven all the way here to attend a party and found Major Crankypants acting the way he had, she'd get the hell out of there too.

She pulled out her cell phone again and scowled down at the screen. Still only one bar of service and a red battery indicator blinked in the corner. Yep. So far, this entire trip had been nothing but a total washout. She'd had high hopes for this story too. Hoped to shed light on what she considered a huge epidemic in the military; their lack of responsiveness toward returning servicemen and women with mental health issues due to their time in battle. She might be too late to help Jaime, her poor brother, but if she could stop even one more soldier from suicide, it would be worth it.

With a sigh, she headed for the diner entrance. No choice but to go inside and beg to make a call. Maybe, if she was lucky, they might still be serving some of those root beer floats advertised on their sign as today's special.

The cool interior of the restaurant felt like heaven on earth to her sunburned skin and Geneva slowly wandered over to the deserted lunch counter. A petite woman stood behind it with her back to the restaurant. She had long, dark hair secured in a braid that reached her waist and wore a bright pink T-shirt emblazoned across the back with the shop's slogan, "Get your Scoops On!"

Geneva slid onto a stool and cleared her throat. "Excuse me?"

"Oh!" The woman whirled to face her and smiled, her expression slightly stunned. She was gorgeous, with her almond-shaped eyes and mocha-colored skin. The same skin tone as Mr. Uncooperative from out in the parking lot. Like any good reporter, Geneva had done her research about Mark before coming to Ortega. This must be the guy's sister. She returned the woman's smile and narrowed her gaze. Maybe there was more than one way to get inside this story. "Sorry. I didn't hear anyone come in," the woman said. "Welcome to Scoops. How may I help you today?"

"I'd love some water please and maybe a root beer float if you still have some left." Geneva smiled back before nodding toward the woman's ice cream cone shaped nametag. "Leila. Pretty name."

"Thank you." A wedding ring glinted on Leila's left hand as she swiped it across her forehead. "It was my grandmother's name. And I'm sorry, but we're all out of root beer. Had quite a crowd earlier." Her smile faltered slightly and she stepped aside to reveal a half-eaten birthday cake on the prep shelf behind her. "We had a private party."

"Oh, right," Geneva said. "I think I met the guest of honor in the parking lot."

"Mark?" Leila snorted. "My condolences."

"How about a piece of birthday cake then?" Geneva hiked her chin toward the dessert.

"Sure thing." Leila sliced Geneva off a generous portion of the three-tiered triple fudge cake and placed it before her along with a frosty glass of ice water. "Glad someone appreciates my hard work. Lord knows my brother didn't."

"Yeah. He seemed kind of grumpy about the whole thing." Geneva took a bite of the luscious dessert and damned near died from ecstasy. The rich chocolate melted in her mouth and the slight bite of the bittersweet fudge cake added just the right counterbalance to all the sugary frosting. "This is fantastic!"

"Thanks." Leila wiped down the bar beside Geneva. "Old family recipe."

"Are you from Ortega originally?"

"Well, my brother and I were born here but our mother is from Samoa."

"Interesting. Your dad Samoan too?"

"No. American." Her abrupt tone effectively slammed the door on that topic.

All righty then. Daddy issues.

Geneva took a few more bites of cake before trying again. "Wow. I've never met an islander before, other than Hawaiian."

Leila laughed. "Yeah. Everyone guesses African-American or Latina or even Chinese. No one ever guesses Pacific Islander."

"Well, I'm all for diversity." Geneva flipped her dark red curls over her shoulder and smiled. "Me? I'm Mexican and Irish."

"Nice." Leila finished wiping down the area, then helped herself to a piece of cake and took a seat beside Geneva at the counter. The place was all but empty except for a table out on the deck. Geneva couldn't make out their faces, backlit as they were against the afternoon sunshine, just their silhouettes.

Leila downed half her cake in a few bites, and then took a sip of her water. "So, what brings you to Ortega? Do you live around here or are you just visiting?"

"I actually live up in the Bay Area. I came here for my work, but my car died in your parking lot and my cell's dead. I was hoping maybe I could use your phone."

"Absolutely." Leila finished what was left of her cake then took her dishes behind the counter before grabbing the store's cordless phone off its cradle on the wall. "Help yourself."

Geneva finished her food and water while Leila started taking down the decorations for her brother's party. The diner was nice, with its slightly retro décor and sparkling clean surfaces. A seagull swooped down onto the railing leading out to the deck, its lonely caw reminding Geneva of the last time she and her brother had been to the beach. Jaime had just gotten home from his last tour in Afghanistan and had been finishing his debriefing at Army headquarters in Arlington, Virginia. The weather had been perfect then too, all blue skies and warm, gentle breezes. Two months later, Jaime was dead.

"I'm surprised Mark didn't help you out," Leila said, breaking Geneva out of her reverie before the painful lump in her throat turned to something more. The woman balanced precariously on a chair to reach some streamers taped to the ceiling. Geneva felt compelled to rush over and hold the thing steady for her. "He's a sucker for a damsel in distress."

"He wasn't exactly friendly. More like frigid," Geneva said, staring up at Leila as she held the chair still. "Especially after he found out what I do."

Leila pulled down a wad of crepe paper and tossed it to the floor. "What do you do?"

"I'm a reporter. For the National Tribune."

"Oh." Leila chuckled. "Yeah, I'm not surprised my brother didn't want to talk to you then. He's not big on the media these days. Or ever, really. Thinks they're all liars. Doesn't help they've been swarming around here like vultures near roadkill either." Leila winced. "Sorry. Bad choice of words. I suppose you're here about the recent deaths too."

"The suicides? Yeah, I am. But that's a pretty broad brush to paint an entire industry with. Not all reporters lie. Most of us subscribe to the Journalistic Code of Ethics." Geneva grabbed a trash bag off the counter and stuffed the discarded crepe paper into it. Never mind in her boss's case, it was kind of true. Geneva was cut from different cloth. Her cause was just. "Your brother doesn't even know me."

"Oh, don't take it personally. It's not about you." Leila climbed down, moved the chair a few feet to the left, and then climbed up again to grab more decorations. "With Mark, it's about what happened when we were growing up."

Inside, Geneva gave a silent fist-pump. She'd known those daddy issues were involved somehow. "What happened?"

"Suffice it to say our dad was a consummate liar," Leila said. "Never could tell the truth about anything. So now Mark goes into any conversation expecting the same."

"That sounds like an awful way to live," Geneva said, sensing there was more to the story. This Mark guy sounded like a real piece of work. And people called *her* cynical. She snorted. "I bet his attitude caused some waves over the years."

"You have no idea," Leila said, nose wrinkled. "If you want to talk to my brother, know this. He judges the world and everyone in it by his own set of high standards and no one can ever measure up. It's almost like he enjoys living his life in perpetual disappointment and alone."

"How sad," Geneva said.

"What's sad?" a deep male voice asked from the shadows.

Geneva turned to see the people from out on the deck walk back inside the diner, one of which was Mark in all his tall, buff, half-naked glory. He watched her with those gorgeous gray-green eyes, his muscled arms crossed over his rock-hard chest. Despite Geneva's current opinion of him, a warm tingle started low in her core. She'd never found the whole shaved-head look attractive before, but this guy made her seriously reconsider her life choices.

Not helpful, girl. Not at all.

Flustered, she fiddled with the trash bag, suddenly not sure what to do with her hands. Mark kept right on staring at her and she got the eerie feeling he could see right through to her soul with those haunting eyes of his. Finally, she gave up any pretense of being busy and headed toward the counter to escape his too-knowing gaze. "I, uh, need to use the phone."

One side of Mark's full lips quirked upward in a sure-you-do smirk.

"She's helping me with the decorations." Leila stepped down off her chair and faced her brother down even though he towered above her and had her size-wise by at least one-hundred fifty pounds. Geneva couldn't help but admire the woman's gumption. "Remember?" Leila placed her hands on her hips and scowled. "The same decorations you didn't give a shit about."

"Look, LeLi," Mark said, his tone conciliatory despite his defensive stance. "I'm sorry about the party. But you know how I feel—"

"What I know is that you acted like a spoiled, pompous ass." Leila poked her finger into his chest for emphasis, not backing down an inch. Geneva stifled a grin. Like David telling off Goliath. She liked Leila more by the second. Her relationship with Mark reminded Geneva of her relationship with Jaime, before…

A sharp pang of sadness stabbed Geneva's chest and she swallowed hard against the unexpected sting of tears. Four months gone and the pain still felt as sharp as the day the Highway Patrol had shown up at her front door to relay the horrific news of what had happened. Sometimes at night, when she closed her eyes, Geneva could still see the pity in the officer's eyes, smell the faint stench of raw fish from the open market just a few blocks down from her apartment, as they'd stood on her tiny front porch and she'd heard the words that had changed her life forever.

Ma'am, I'm sorry to report that your brother, Jaime Rios, committed suicide…

Geneva gave herself a hard, mental shake and did her best to focus on the present. Now wasn't the time to get all sappy again about what happened. Now was the time to get the story she needed to break into the world arena of journalism and expose the military's huge mistake where her brother and so many others were concerned.

She'd failed Jaime once already. She wouldn't do it again.

Leila continued to lay into Mark despite his irritated frown. "…and after mom went through all that trouble to make your favorite cake too. Don't give me that shit about your trust issues, little bro. It's time for you to get the hell over it, mister."

Geneva bit her lips to keep from laughing out loud and met Mark's gaze with a raised brow. *Take that, Major Crankypants.*

"Tough standards are the only thing that keep this world going," he said to his sister, then turned to Geneva. "Can I talk to you outside for a moment, please?"

CHAPTER FOUR

"What the hell were you doing in there?" Mark led Geneva back out into the parking lot, keeping a solid grip on her arm the entire time.

"I told you I had to use the phone." She tried to free herself from his grip and then gave him an annoyed look when she couldn't. "Then I had some cake and helped your sister clean up. Why?"

"Hey, Aleki," Leila called from the entrance behind them. "Be nice. She's okay."

Mark waved his sister off and led Geneva over to where her SUV sat alone in the corner of the lot. "You're leaving."

"Hard to do when my car won't start." She tried to pull away from him again and this time he let her go. Geneva crossed her arms, which only highlighted her magnificent rack again. Not that Mark was looking. Definitely not. "My cell was out of juice so I went inside to use the phone. Sue me. And I thought your name was Mark."

"Aleki is my middle name." Jaw clenched, he attempted to stare her down. Except she wasn't backing down any more than his sister had. Seems he was losing his intimidating touch. Not that he'd ever had much of one to begin with, especially when ladies were involved. Still, the sooner he got rid of Geneva Rios, the sooner he could get to the courthouse and get on with his plans for the rest of the day. He sighed and cocked his chin toward her vehicle. "Pop the hood."

Geneva stared at him a moment before walking around to the driver's side of the SUV and doing as he asked, cursing under her breath the entire time. Sure enough, the whole distributor cap assemblage was a mess. He was no Jace when it came to mechanics, but he knew enough to fix it. Still barefoot and in his wetsuit shorts, naked from the waist up, he leaned over the engine and got to work. Given her profession, he wouldn't have put it past her to put everything back the wrong way as another attempt to get him to talk. "These distributors can be tricky."

"Tell me about it." Geneva's disgruntled tone was laced with fatigue and suddenly Mark felt something he wasn't prepared for where she was concerned. Sympathy. He did his best to stifle the unwanted emotion, though it continued to bubble inside him. "I don't even know any local mechanics," she huffed.

"There's a shop about a mile from here. Burrell's. My buddy, Jace works there part-time. Want me to call him out to take a look?" Mark placed his hands on his hips and squinted into the late afternoon sun. He still didn't trust Geneva any farther than he could see her. She was a part of the media, after all, and he'd dealt with enough of them lately to last him a lifetime. Plus, the last thing he needed was some nosy snoop messing up his plans for his own quiet investigation into the recent SEAL deaths. Most reporters he knew were about as subtle as a nuclear warhead. His well-honed honor, though, wouldn't let him walk away from her distress either. Lord knew if Leila or his mom were in the same position, he'd want a Good Samaritan to help them out too. "I think I can get this working for you again. Might not be a bad idea to have Burrell's check it out before you head home, though."

"Home?" Geneva stood several feet to the side of him, her hand shielding her eyes from the sun as she watched his every move. A strange tingle spread over his skin from her stare, as if her gaze were more of a physical caress. She gave a curt nod. "Thanks. But I'm not heading home until I get what I came here for."

Mark scowled and shook off his odd attraction for this frustrating woman. Yes, she was hot, in an Eva Mendes sort of way. But he was not going there. Not now and not with her. She was a reporter. He didn't talk to reporters. No matter how delectable said reporter might appear. God, did she paint on those denim cutoffs or what? Hugging all her curves and cupping that fine ass like his own fingers itched to do.

Sighing, Mark turned back to the vehicle again.

It had been too long since he'd gotten laid. That had to be it.

He tinkered with the wires on the distributor cap some more.

Besides, he had enough on his plate with his security training business and making sure his mom's and his sister's restaurants ran smoothly. Then there was the fact all his recent relationships ended up the same anyway. Most of the women he'd dated since leaving the Navy said he was too demanding, said that his standards were too high, and that he was looking for a saint, not a girlfriend.

Much as Mark hated to admit it, Leila hadn't been lying. He did have trust issues. And given Geneva's line of work and her persistence in wanting to interview him, those weren't likely to go away anytime soon. He frowned and fiddled with a few hoses, then straightened. "Try to start it."

"Seriously? You think you fixed it that fast?" Geneva gave him a skeptical look, but slid in behind the wheel just the same. Mark stepped back as she cranked the engine. The SUV started right up. She leaned out the open door and gave him a small, reluctant smile. For some reason, his afternoon brightened considerably. "Thanks."

"No problem." Mark closed the hood then wiped his hands on his neoprene shorts. "Easy fix. Couple of crossed wires. Like I said, get it checked out before you leave Ortega though."

Geneva exited the vehicle once more and stood beside him, the car still running. This close, he caught a whiff of her perfume on the afternoon breeze—orange blossom and cloves on a sun-kissed woman. The sea wind stirred loose strands of her hair around her face, making her look softer and younger than the hard-edged, hard-boiled reporter she tried to portray. "Are you sure you won't change your mind about letting me interview you?" she asked, narrowing her gaze. "I won't let up until you do, you know. This story needs to be told. The US military is failing these guys."

"Well, at least that's a new angle from the one I heard from the other reporters. All they seemed to care about was exploiting these guys' families and pasts. Splashing their pain and suffering all over the front pages." Of course, they'd all been upfront about their motives too—selling more papers. But from the brittle edge to Geneva's tone, this sounded more personal to her, which made the whole prospect more worrisome. "Why is this so important to you?"

She gave him some serious side-eye, that flicker of darkness reappearing in her gaze again before vanishing. "I'm patriotic."

"Right." A mix of intrigue and trepidation gurgled inside Mark. He sensed a deep core of pain beneath Geneva's surface, which she seemed to try to cover with a stiff layer of pessimism and prickliness. Still, he wasn't sure he'd ever be able to trust her completely, and these guys she wanted him to talk about were his comrades, they'd fought side-by-side in more warzones than he could count. And sure, the country's VA system needed a huge overhaul, no doubt about it but to prove their deaths had been more than suicides would take time and finesse. So far, all she'd shown him was her talent for spouting off sarcasm and bullshit with the best of them.

"Man, you ready to head back home?" Jace yelled as he and Vann exited the diner and walked over to Geneva's SUV. "We got that class downtown at five for the highway patrol."

"What kind of business do you run?" Geneva asked, smiling sweetly at Jace. The guy was an adorable mutt. His nickname in their SEAL unit had been Heinz 57 because he was part Eskimo, part Irish, German, and even a little English and Chinese thrown in for flavor. Whatever his ethnic heritage, the ladies dug Jace and he dug them right back. Mark couldn't suppress a hint of jealousy.

"Brothers In Arms Security runs eight-week courses for law enforcement and business professionals," Vann answered, his voice the equivalent of a brick wall, his secrets guarded tighter than Fort Knox. His stoic expression did little to hide the blatant suspicion in his black eyes. "But since you're a reporter, you probably already knew that, Ms. Rios."

"You told him?" She glanced at Mark.

He shrugged. "What? Like it's a secret?"

"Glad to see I was the topic of conversation over your lunch." Her tone said the exact opposite. She gave Mark a sour look. "So, you train cops and tycoons. To do what? Blow more money on silly classes they don't need?"

"The first half of our course deals with situational awareness, how not to be a target," Jace said, seemingly oblivious to the undercurrent of tension sizzling in the air. "The second half of the course teaches basic survival skills on everything from kidnapping to environmental emergencies. Even viral doomsday scenarios."

"Like a Zombie Apocalypse, you mean?" she asked, her tone smartass.

"It's not as far-fetched as you'd think," Mark said, forcing himself to remain patient. "As a reporter I'd think you'd know never to knock something before you experience it yourself." He eyed her up and down then narrowed his gaze, issuing a challenge. "If you're so gung-ho to write this story, why don't you join us for tonight's class? If you think you're up for it."

"But, man, we're—" Jace started before Geneva cut him off.

"Yeah?" The spark of determination in her eyes made the zing of awareness buzzing inside Mark flare hotter. He tamped it down deep before it got out of hand. There was too much riding on this now, too much time and effort on his part put into investigating the deaths and proving they weren't suicides, for him to start thinking with his cock instead of his brain. No way would she go through with his class tonight. She'd learn her lesson and be on her way home, and Mark would once again be alone here in Ortega, happy as a clam. Just the way he liked it.

"You got yourself a deal," she said, surprising him. She held out a hand for Mark to shake, and then turned back to Jace. "Five pm, you said?"

"Yep. Make sure you wear sturdy boots." Jace started toward the company's camo Hummer parked near the front door of Scoops. He opened the passenger door, grabbed a notepad and pen from the glove compartment, and then scribbled down an address for her as he returned to their group. "Tallest building in downtown Ortega. You can't miss it."

"Great. And I've always got my boots on." She lifted what looked like an expensive, custom-made hiking boot in Jace's direction and smiled before glancing at Mark. "Not sure what boots and tall buildings have to do with anything, but okay."

"You'll find out, Ms. Rios." Vann lingered a moment longer, appraising Geneva with a narrowed gaze. Mark would lay good money Vann would run a full background check on her before the night was over. Nice to know his buddies had his back.

"Mark, you coming?" Jace asked as he climbed behind the wheel of the huge camo-colored Humvee.

"Nah." Mark glanced at Geneva then waved at the guys. "Go ahead. I've got that errand to run. I'll meet you there later."

CHAPTER FIVE

The courthouse in Ortega had been built in the late 1800s and featured the typical Spanish style so prevalent in California, right down to its red tiled roof and white stucco walls.

Mark jogged up the short flight of steps and into the hacienda-esque lobby area. The public records office was near the back of the building, so he started down the long tiled hall, saying hello to several residents as he passed.

He'd stopped by his house to shower and change first before heading over there. If he made good time, he hoped to get copies of the death certificates and take them back to the compound to go over with the guys. Luckily, when he walked into the public records office, there was no line and the cute clerk he'd been hoping would be on duty sat at her desk behind the counter.

Mark took a deep breath and plastered on what he hoped was his most charming smile before striding confidently up to the counter. "Hello."

The clerk's eyes widened slightly as she looked at him, a slight blush rising in her cheeks. He put her at late twenties, close to his own age, maybe a little older. No ring that he could see. Perhaps once this whole mess with the mysterious deaths was over, he'd come back and ask her out. Ortega was small and despite a lot of tourist traffic, finding cute, eligible local girls to date was harder than you'd think.

She cleared her throat and ran her hand down the front of her pink top before pushing to her feet. That's when he saw it. A fairly prominent baby bump. Okay, maybe dating wouldn't be an option. Not that he was against a relationship with a single mom, but he guessed a brand new romantic entanglement was the last thing on her mind right now. She stepped closer to the counter. "How may I help you today?"

"I need to see a couple of death certificates, please." Mark rattled off the names then waited while she typed them into her computer. Most of the bigger cities had made all this available digitally, but little Ortega was still catching up with the modern era.

"Yes. I see those here." She glanced from her screen to him, her smile falling into a frown. "These have been popular items lately."

"Really?" Mark fished his wallet out of his back pocket. He'd like to say he was surprised, but given the media coverage over Rick and Jon's deaths, he wasn't. He sniffed and leaned his forearms on the counter and glanced at the clerk's name placard. Louise. "Lots of reporters, huh, Louise?"

"Yeah." She stood and pushed her chair in. "It will take me just a minute to pull these. You can have a seat if you want."

"Great. Thanks." Mark walked over to a pair of chairs against the wall and plopped down into one. At least this would give him a chance to sort through some of his emails. Lord knew he hadn't had a chance to even open his laptop since last night. Most of what filled his inbox was junk or more birthday wishes. The junk he trashed. The birthday wishes he filed away for later.

Once his mailbox was cleaned out, he tapped over to his Internet browser. Ortega might still be in the dark ages, paperwork-wise, but they'd at least installed free Wi-Fi in all their public spaces. Brothers In Arms had pitched in a large donation to help with that too. With his thumb, he typed in National Tribune into the search box and hit Enter. Soon his screen filled with links to the newspaper's website. Clicking on the main page, he hit the Staff button on the top menu. There, under a Reporters tab, he found Geneva's pic and a short bio. Nothing he didn't already know, but it would be good to keep tabs on her in case she published something about him or Ortega on the fly. Finally, he found the sign-up page for their daily email newsletter and entered his work address.

"Here we are," Louise said, returning from a back room. "So sad what happened to them."

"Yeah." Mark stepped up to the counter once more and briefly scanned the two certificates to make sure they were the right ones then handed them back to Louise. Time to turn on that charm again. "They used to work for me. We served in Afghanistan together. Like brothers. I own Brothers In Arms."

"Oh dear." Louise put a comforting hand on his forearm. "I recognized you the minute you walked in here, Mr. Rogers. I'm so sorry for your loss."

"Thanks." Mark exhaled. "I don't suppose there's any way I could get copies of these without you recording it. A copy of the autopsy reports would be amazing too." If the cops got wind of what he suspected, they'd take over the case and all his hard work would drown in a sea of government red tape.

Louise blinked. "Normally copies of the certificates are ten dollars each and I'd have to process the transaction through the computer. The autopsy reports would require you to fill out a request then a few days for us to process."

"I know." He nodded and frowned down at the counter top. "I just thought with all this media frenzy, we could avoid any more sensationalism and profit over their deaths. Their families have been through so much already."

The clerk's brows drew together and she swallowed hard. "You're right. You and your guys do so much for this town. It's the least I can do. Hang tight a minute."

"Sure thing." Mark watched while she took the death certificates back into the file room then returned a few moments later with a sealed manila envelope in her hand.

"Here you are, Mr. Rogers. I think you'll find everything you need in there."

"Thanks, Louise." He smiled. "When are you due?"

"December," she said, her expression glowing. "My fiancé's in the Marines. He gets out in November, so just in time."

"Perfect." Mark tapped the edge of the envelope on the counter then turned to leave. "Thanks again, Louise."

"Any time, Mr. Rogers."

Mark hurried back out to his black Jeep Wrangler and climbed into the driver's seat to head toward the Brothers In Arms compound on the edge of town. There were still about an hour before they needed to leave to get downtown to set up for the night's class and he wanted to go over these certificates with the guys.

He, Vann and Jace had pooled their money together and purchased the forty-acre property after they were discharged. The compound was huge and had everything they needed—beach access for water rescue training, flatlands for desert scenarios, foothills for hiking and wilderness training, even an old, two-story, Victorian-style farmhouse near the edge of the vineyards bordering their property. That farmhouse was where Mark lived. There were also separate buildings for their office, storage, and even a small arena area where they had students practice their hand-to-hand combat skills.

Twenty minutes later, he pulled up into his parking spot in the gravel lot of the compound and climbed out of his door-less vehicle. Jace and Vann were outside the storage building loading up the back of the Humvee with gear for the class.

"Hey, man," Jace called raising a hand in greeting. "You stop at the courthouse?"

"Yep," Mark said, passing by them and heading into his office.

The guys soon joined him.

He ripped open the top of the envelope and found the two death certificates inside along with the thick autopsy reports. He handed Rick's set to the guys and started perusing Jon's himself. "See if you find anything suspicious in there."

Unfortunately, after an hour of searching, he'd found nothing out of the ordinary in Jon's report. Per the findings, the guy had shot himself in the head on the coastal cliffs then tumbled down the side of the rocks into the Pacific. All the findings were consistent with that, including his plunge into the ocean afterward. No weird bullet angles, no trace of alcohol or drugs in his system at the time of death. No nothing.

Shit. Mark scrubbed a hand over his face and sighed.

His instincts told him neither Rick nor Jon would ever kill themselves like that.

Granted, he was no pathologist, but he knew the doctor who served as Ortega's medical examiner and the woman was thorough. Still, there had to be something they were missing. He glanced over at Vann and Jace. "You guys find anything?"

"Not really," Jace said. "The trajectory of the bullet from Rick's gun is right logistically to support a self-inflicted gunshot wound to the head."

Leave it to the mechanic to highlight the engineering portion of the case.

Vann continued to scowl down at the autopsy report in his hands. "There's no drugs of any kind found in Rick's system."

"Yeah." Mark rubbed his hand over the top of his head. His hair was starting to grow back in again. He'd need another shave soon. "Same here with Jon's. Nothing to go on there."

"No." Vann looked up, his dark gaze concerned. "I mean there were no drugs in his system, but that's not possible. I know for a fact he took at least three prescription meds daily. One painkiller for his back injury. One to lower his cholesterol. And one for anti-anxiety for his PTSD. There should've been trace amounts of all three in his system at the time of his death."

"Maybe they don't screen for regular medications?" Jace offered.

"No." Mark frowned. "Dr. Gerber told me once that toxicology done post-mortem screens for everything, that way they can rule out a fatal overdose." He sat back in his seat and crossed his arms. "Do you think maybe Rick just didn't take his meds that day? If his levels were off, that might indicate why he was off mentally."

"Even if he missed a day, there should still be traces in his bloodstream." Vann handed the report to Mark. "My guess is the bloodwork, at least, was faked."

"Fuck." A rush of both relief and dread flooded Mark's system. Relief that there was a shred of proof he was right that the deaths weren't suicides. Dread that if they pursued this, they'd be opening a whole can of worms where the cases were concerned and exposing themselves as targets to whoever was responsible. "We can't say anything about this to anyone right now. Not until we're sure."

"Right." Jace nodded. "We need more proof."

"Agreed," Vann said. "What're we going to do now?"

Mark stood and walked to the windows on the far side of his office. Geneva had already made the connection between the two dead SEALs and his business. She was smart, tenacious. Wouldn't take much more for her to connect the rest of these dots either. Much as Mark hated to admit it, the safest thing for him to do was to keep her close and monitor her activities. He'd worked too hard for too many years to build Brothers In Arms into what it was today. He damned sure wouldn't let it all come crashing down because of some nosy reporter raising suspicions about his former employees' mental stability. Yes, those guys had issues after they'd come home, but hell no would they have killed themselves. First though, he needed to make sure he could trust her. Mark glanced back over at his buddies and grinned. "Don't know about you guys, but I've got a building to tackle."

CHAPTER SIX

"Lean back and let go of the scaffolding," Mark said from above, his smile reassuring.

Geneva wanted to; she did, except when she'd accepted his invitation tonight, she'd expected to watch a bunch of ordinary people being put through what amounted to a boot camp. Never in a million years had she imagined hanging over the edge of a ten-story building in downtown Ortega.

At this altitude, a constant brisk wind smacked her hard in the face and her hair kept coming loose from beneath the helmet they'd strapped on her head. If she wasn't so stubborn—clear down to her bones, as her parents always used to say—she would've told Mark to forget it and bring her back up on the roof.

Unfortunately, though, Geneva was no quitter. So, here she hung, glancing down at the very hard, very distant concrete sidewalk below. "Are you sure this stuff will hold me?"

"Yes, I promise." Mark nodded from beneath his orange hardhat. "Tested all the ropes and carabiners myself. They're idiot-proof."

As if to prove his point, one of the patrol officers, a portly guy who looked more like Santa than a servant of the law, skittered down the wall beside her like he was walking in the park.

"See?" Mark hiked his chin toward the guy. "If he can do it, so can you." Santa, Jr. waved and chuckled at her as he sped past Geneva on his way to the ground. "C'mon. I've got other guys waiting to use your lines."

Damn.

Geneva closed her eyes and took a deep breath, hoping to psych herself up for what appeared to be certain death. *If you're there, Jaime. A little help please.*

"Just tell your body what to do," Mark said, his voice steady and calm. "Now go."

Inch by inch, she lowered herself; hand over hand, eyes closed and heart pounding. She'd interviewed convicted killers, conducted sting operations on crooked politicians, even gone undercover in a rat-infested crack house. None of that had been even half as terrifying as this.

Before she knew it, however, arms reached up to grab her and Mark's two partners guided her the last few feet to the ground. Safe. She was safe. She winked up at the sky above. *Thanks, Jaime.* Her job might require staunch disbelief and her usual outer attitude might be cynical to the core, but her heart and soul still needed some anchor to hope and wonder.

"Good job, Geneva," Jace said, helping her off with her harness. "That wasn't so bad, was it?"

Peering up to the rooftop of the building, Geneva spotted Mark giving her a thumbs-up and pride mixed with no small amount of attraction flooded her system. She'd never, ever, pictured herself doing something so crazy. Yet, she had. Imagine that. "No. Not so bad after all."

"Take a seat over there with the others." Vann pointed to where the rest of the group was gathered near a water cooler, his demeanor business-like as always. "We've still got a few more runs before we're done."

Geneva nodded. She usually had a magic touch where men were concerned, getting them to talk about all sorts of things they normally kept hidden—a talent she used to her advantage as a reporter. Vann, though, seemed like a conundrum wrapped inside a sturdy wall of nope.

She joined the rest of the group of participants. Didn't matter. Her real mission here was getting to Mark Rogers. Maybe Jace too, if she could pin him down long enough for an interview. He'd been friendly enough to her tonight. Geneva made her way to the water cooler set up on the back bumper of the Humvee, nodding vague acknowledgments to the officers around her, her knees still wobbly and her pulse still racing. Hard as scaling down the side of that building had been, she felt exhilarated, triumphant, damned near giddy.

"Quite a rush, eh?" Someone patted her on the back. "You from around here, miss?"

"Bay Area," Geneva said between sips of water. It was Santa, Jr.

"Ortega's a fine town," he said. Lord, the guy even had a white beard. Geneva bet he made a boatload of cash renting himself out for parties once the holidays rolled around. "Been here all my life," Santa, Jr. said. "And you won't find better trainers than these boys here at Brothers In Arms."

"Are you a personal friend of theirs?" She took a seat on the curb and invited the officer to sit next to her. "I'm just passing through."

"Oh, I've known the Rogers family for years. Hard times their mom had after their no-good dad left them. The kids were real young," Santa shook his head. "Hear he lives in Phoenix now, the deadbeat."

"Hmm." Geneva wanted to ask more about Mark's father, but didn't want to blow what rapport she had with the guy by being too pushy. "His mom still lives here though?"

"Yep. Sefina runs a restaurant not too far from here, called Aiga's. That's the Samoan word for family."

"Interesting." From seeing Mark interact with his sister back at Scoops and hearing a little about what happened with his parents, it was understandable why he was so close with the family he had left. Geneva's heart pinched unexpectedly as thoughts of her brother flooded her mind once more. She and Jaime had been close too. They both lived out here on the west coast while their parents had stayed back east in Virginia. She hadn't been home to visit in years. In fact, the last time she'd seen her parents had been at Jaime's funeral. She swallowed hard against the lump in her throat and frowned down at her plastic cup of water, doing her best to stay focused on her conversation with Santa. "What about—"

"Geronimo!" Mark yelled from where he dangled at the top of the building before hurtling to the ground at breakneck speed. He stopped a few feet short from the sidewalk to gasps and applause from the students. "Thanks everyone for coming out tonight. Next time, we'll be doing wilderness training. Have a good week."

Geneva shook off the odd tension filling her muscles and quickening her pulse. For a moment, all she could picture was Mark plummeting to his death, and it left her strangely… *terrified.* Seeing a man die would be horrific, and the fact that man would be Mark only increased the strange, heart-squeezing pressure in her chest.

She shook off the weird feelings and pushed to her feet. She'd been on the road all morning and hadn't taken a break yet. That had to be the reason for her odd connection to a man she'd only met hours earlier.

The guys were gathering up and stowing their equipment in the back of the Humvee and she pitched in to help. Seemed the least she could do after they'd given her the most amazing time of her life thus far, even if Mark and Vann still looked at her as if she were toxic waste.

Geneva hazarded a glance at Mark, that distracting warm tingle inside her spreading out from her core to her extremities. Honestly, the guy *was* built like a Greek god and had a smile that hinted at all sorts of wicked adventures, and she wouldn't be diametrically opposed to some exciting times ahead between the two of them, perhaps even some between the sheets action. There was no doubt in her mind Mr. Mark Rogers could take her to new heights there as well. But first though, she needed to get inside his head, get his opinion on those recent deaths. Then, maybe, they could learn more about each other in different...*areas*. Besides, she found she wasn't quite ready for their night to end despite her fatigue. "So, what do you guys do after class ends?"

"Back to the office for me," Vann said, his voice abrupt. He gave Geneva a warning look before returning his attention to their students. Right. The guy was protective of Mark. Good to remember.

"Jeez, some manners would be nice, bro," Jace said. "Don't mind him, Geneva. Vann's just pissed because he had to work the bottom tonight. Guy loves being up in the clouds."

"To answer your question." Mark pushed between his buddies to toss a bundle of ropes and equipment into the back of the Humvee. "We usually hang out. Sometimes I head back to the compound to finish up paperwork or whatever."

"Oh." His response hadn't exactly been an open invitation, but still there was a little wiggle room and Geneva took all the opportunities she could find. She leaned against the side of the vehicle as they finished loading their stuff, and Vann slammed the back of the Humvee closed. "Anybody want to grab a bite to eat?" she asked. "Since I'm new here, I don't really know any good places."

"Can't," Vann said, climbing into the driver's seat of the Humvee.

Jace backed slowly toward the sidewalk once more, exchanging a look with Mark. "Wish I could, but I need to double-check for any forgotten gear, then I'm pulling a shift at the garage tonight. Maybe next time though." He waved to Geneva then disappeared into the lobby of the bank building again.

Which left her and Mark. He stood like a statue beside her—a gorgeous, skeptical statue, but still—arms crossed and gaze narrowed. "Why do you really want to have dinner with me?"

"Besides the fact I'm starving?" She raised an eyebrow. "Fine. I thought maybe we could talk some more. Get to know each other better." At his sigh, she held up her hands. "No strings attached and no questions about my story, I promise. Plus, it will give me a chance to thank you for an incredible experience tonight."

"Huh." One side of his full lips quirked into a cocky smile. "I usually only hear that the morning after."

"Wow." Geneva shook her head. "Humble too."

"Hey, I'm just being honest." He checked his watch. He'd changed into black jeans and company polo since she'd seen him earlier at the ice cream shop and still looked fresh as clean laundry. She, on the other hand, felt a bit dirty, shaken and generally disconcerted after her trek down Ortega's tallest building.

"Scoops should still be open," Mark said, "if you want to head there."

"Let's do it." She fished her keys out of her pocket and headed for her SUV.

"See you later at the office?" Vann called to Mark as he started the Humvee.

"Nah," Mark turned back to Geneva and smiled. Sincere or not, she felt that grin all the way to her toes. "We're going to grab some dinner at Leila's. I'll probably head home after that. See you tomorrow."

CHAPTER SEVEN

An hour later, Mark and Geneva sat at a back table at Scoops. Thankfully, his sister had been too busy to do more than take their orders after they'd come in, so he wasn't subjected to the usual sibling interrogations he got whenever he went out on a date.

His thoughts stopped short. This was not a date.

This was business. Nothing more.

A way to find out more about Geneva and this story she felt compelled to write.

And yes, she'd more than proven herself back at the training and yes; even Mark had to say he was impressed with her courage. Still didn't mean he was ready to bare his soul to a woman he hardly knew.

One of the waiters brought over their lemon sodas and Geneva put down her phone at last. Apparently, she'd had a chance to charge it up on the drive to Leila's place and now it all but monopolized her attention. Typical of the reporters he'd met. He shook his head. Always rooting around for their next angle.

"Can I ask you something?" She set her phone aside then took a cookie wafer from the top of her soda and bit into it. Mark did his best not to notice the trace of whipped cream dotting her upper lip or his crazy urge to lick it off.

Damn. His libido was seriously out of control.

"I suppose." He took a long swig of his soda. The tangy lemon and fizz of the soda water tickled his nose, distracting him from the knot of unexpected lust for Geneva in the pit of his gut. "Doesn't mean I have to answer, right?"

Geneva gave him an irritated look. "What do you make of all these deaths?"

"Which ones?" He was being deliberately obtuse, but he didn't care.

"The SEALs." She gave him a don't-be-a-smartass look. "Besides the two retired SEALs who worked for you, there was another guy who was still active-duty, home on leave."

"What about them?"

"Are you going to answer every one my questions with another question?"

He opened his mouth to give another sarcastic response then stopped as he caught sight of the TV in the corner. Another commercial for that entitled asshole Frank Sutton. Mark gave a disgusted snort and downed more of his soda. Bastard was an ex-SEAL, but didn't deserve to wear the title. He'd damned near washed out during Hell Week and only served his required enlistment before getting out.

Normally, Mark would've said good riddance. Except now, Sutton was running for Congress and using his former Navy SEAL status to woo people's votes. The end of the commercial said it was sponsored by some super PAC calling themselves, The American Way Group. More like racist, bigoted bastards group, at least from what Mark had read. They believed the country belonged in the hands of those they considered to be true Americans—white men.

"What's wrong?" Geneva frowned, swiveling to see the TV behind her. "Oh, that guy."

"Sutton's an idiot," Mark grumbled.

"Tell me how you really feel." Geneva faced him again with a grin. "What don't you like about him?"

"There aren't enough hours in the day." Mark chuckled. "Trust me."

"How about you trust me?"

He gave her a long look. *Gaining my trust takes time, sweetheart, and you haven't earned it yet.* No way was he spilling his guts about his true feelings regarding his comrades' deaths. He swallowed hard against the tension knotting his throat. Especially with what he and the guys had found in those autopsy reports earlier, confirming his suspicions those deaths weren't suicides at all. So instead, he concentrated on the topic at hand, hoping to distract her and himself too. "I don't like Frank Sutton or his backers."

"Why not?" Geneva asked as another waiter delivered their burgers and fries to the table. "He's an ex-SEAL, right? I thought you guys had some kind of eternal brotherhood."

"For those people who join for the right reasons, yeah we do." He picked up the ketchup and squirted a generous portion on his fries then watched while she did the same. "Frank was never in it for the right reasons."

"Why did he join then? From what I've heard the training alone would be enough to deter anyone who didn't want to be there."

"Who knows?" Mark took a huge bite of burger then wiped his mouth. "Fame, prestige, bragging rights. All the above. He got out as soon as he could too. All I remember about the guy back then is he liked to drink and run his mouth. A lot."

"Hmm." Geneva dug into her food with gusto and Mark was glad. He couldn't stand those women who nibbled everything like rabbits. Give him a woman with a healthy appetite any day. "That's weird," she said. "I thought it was a SEAL prerequisite to be a selfless, tough, silent type. One for all and all for one, sort of thing."

"The best of us are, but not Sutton," he said around a bite of fries. "That dumbass used to sit around the mess hall yammering about how bad he wanted to be rich and how the world owed him. He thought he got the shaft because his wealthy daddy lost all his money speculating in real estate. Idiot."

"Interesting." Geneva took another gulp of her lemon soda. "What about his backers? The American Way Group? What did they ever do to you?"

"Me personally?" Mark shrugged, and then finished off his burger before answering. He couldn't see any harm in telling her his thoughts on this subject. After all, the guy was running for public office. Wasn't like Frank Sutton's background was a secret anymore. And those American Way bastards ran their damned TV commercials what seemed like every two seconds. "Well, let's see. Other than they'd like to see America's power returned to a bunch of old white guys who only care about themselves and have no idea what the rest of the people who make up this fine country deal with on a daily basis, you mean?"

"Okay then." She smiled at him after devouring another fry. "Anything else?"

"Sutton's running on a platform that freezes the minimum wage at a sub-standard level, promotes discriminatory policies toward people of color and women, and he'd happily trot us right back into a bunch of wars America has no business being in. That enough?"

"Plenty. So, can we talk about your two former employees now?"

Mark gave her a flat look. "You never quit, do you?"

"Not unless I'm absolutely forced." Geneva shrugged and nibbled another fry. "Besides, I wouldn't be very good at my job if I did, right?"

With a sigh, Mark tapped his fingers on the table. As long as she was in town, he wouldn't get any peace until he talked to her, that much was obvious. He'd had more than enough interviews to last him a lifetime, not including the ones he'd been wrangled into after his last unit in Kabul had been involved in a high-profile firefight. Once he'd arrived back in the states, the reporters had descended like vultures to get his insider's view of what had happened. Jace and Vann had been targeted too, but Mark had taken the brunt as the unit's leader. If anything, at least the experience had taught him to answer only exactly what was asked and to keep your cards close to the vest. Especially with what they'd discovered on Rick's autopsy report earlier. "What do you want to know?"

"How well did you know the victims?"

"You probably know all of this already, but we all served together in Afghanistan. After the war, Rick and Jon both came to work for me at Brothers In Arms as independent contractors. Taught some of our obstacle course classes and self-defense."

"So you were close with them?" Geneva narrowed her gaze.

"Not overly." Mark shrugged. "What's your point?"

"I'm just wondering if there were signs."

"What kind of signs?" He frowned.

"Depression or talk of suicide or anything at all that might've made you think they were in trouble."

Honestly, after Rick's death six months ago and Jon's only two months prior, Mark had thought of nothing else. Guilt had kept him up for a couple of nights, thinking he should've seen something, done something to prevent what had happened. Hell, Rick had two little girls and a loving wife at home and Jon had just gotten engaged a few months prior. That's what had initially started him on his path to the truth about their deaths. They had no reason to want to die and every reason to want to live. Now, after seeing those reports this afternoon, he would make it his mission to prove they'd been murdered.

He swallowed hard against the unease that surfaced when he thought about the battle ahead and the evidence he still needed to collect. He wouldn't be sharing any of that with Geneva though, no matter how well she'd proven herself tonight. If she got wind of what he and the guys had found, she could splash that shit all over her tabloid paper with no regard to the people she hurt by ruining his investigation. The military's life insurance company refused to pay out benefits in cases of suicide. Meaning neither Rick's nor Jon's family had received any benefits. In addition to finding the bastard responsible for killing them, Mark wanted to make sure those family members they'd left behind were well cared for. Geneva blasting out his findings before he had time to get all his ducks in a row evidence-wise could ruin everything. Mark shrugged and slipped her an easy lie. "No. Nothing."

"Huh. Interesting." Geneva pushed her empty food basket away. "Dinner was delicious, by the way."

"Yeah." Mark winked. "Leila makes a mean burger."

"That's not the only thing I'm mean at," his sister said, finally making her way to their table. She turned to Geneva and smiled. "How was everything?"

"Great, thanks."

"Good." Leila gave her brother a stern look. "Take her somewhere nice after this, eh? Weather's lovely tonight. You two should drive up the coast, check out the stars."

"Stop matchmaking, sis. This isn't a date." Mark glanced over at Geneva and noticed pretty pink color rising in her cheeks.

Okay. So, maybe she thought this *was* a date. He wasn't sure how he felt about that. Lord knew he found her attractive and she seemed to like him too. Frustrated now in more ways than one, he crossed his arms and leaned back in his chair, shooting his sister an irritated stare. "Don't you have other customers?"

"Subtlety was never his strong suit." Leila smacked Mark playfully on the bicep then put her arm around him and squeezed him affectionately. "But I love him anyway."

"Love you too, sis." He slung his arm around her waist and hugged her in return before swatting her hard on the butt. "Now go away. We're busy."

Leila stuck her tongue out at him as she walked away.

"What are we busy doing?" Geneva asked as she finished off her soda, batting her eyes at him in a perfect Pollyanna parody. "I wouldn't be opposed to a drive up the coast either, by the way. The trip down here was beautiful. I'd love to see the shoreline at night. If you don't have something else to do, that is."

"Well, in that case." Mark started to pull out his wallet, but she waved him off, handed a passing waiter two twenties, and told him to keep the change. Generous tipper. Another thing he liked in a person. His mom always said if you wanted to know who a person was inside, watch how they treated those who served them. From what he could see of Geneva, she was a decent person. More than decent. "Since you're so interested in my dislike of Frank Sutton and his American Way backers, how about I show you where his top supporters live? That'll give you something to gnaw on."

"Sounds good." She rubbed her flat belly and Mark couldn't help following the movement, suddenly imagining his own hands touching her there, caressing her, making her cry out his name as he pleasured her over and over... *Sweet Jesus on a boogie board.*

Mark pushed to his feet and ran a hand over his head. If he was going to get through this night alive, he needed to get his shit together. Fast.

"I'm stuffed," Geneva said, standing beside him. "Ready?"

"Ready." Mark looked down at her, his stubborn brain still stuck on those erotic images of her in his bed, beneath him, wrapped around him. He shook his head to clear it, and then sighed. "C'mon. It won't take long. It's just a couple of miles up the coast and Leila's right. The views are spectacular. Promise I'll have you home before your bedtime."

"Well, as long as you promise." Her slow smile made a beeline straight to his groin.

CHAPTER EIGHT

Twenty minutes later, they'd left the town limits of Ortega behind and sped down the Pacific Coast Highway heading north in his jeep. Through the open top and sides of his Wrangler, the fresh salt air invigorated Mark like nothing else. God, he loved it near the ocean. At one time, before he'd graduated high school and joined the Navy, he'd dreamed of being a professional surfer, traveling the world for competitions and surfing the planet's best waves. These days, he was happy to find time to do the sport he loved for fun.

He turned off on a small private lane leading into the foothills while Geneva raved about the gorgeous California scenery. Many people didn't appreciate the starkness of the landscape surrounding this area, but Geneva didn't seem to be one of them. Another check in her 'Pros' column.

"Different than the Bay Area, huh?" he asked over the hum of the engine and rush of the wind.

"Yeah. I'm more used to fog and damp. Kind of like London, without the castles." She looked over at him. "You been to San Francisco?"

"Couple times. Flew in and out of there when I was in the military. It's been a few years though."

"You should visit again. I'm sure a lot has changed. I'll show you around."

Anticipation buzzed through Mark's system at her invitation. Of course, he could be reading way too much into it too. He was horny, pure and simple. And she was a stranger. And a reporter. A long shower and some one-handed relief later would be his wisest choice.

They rounded a curve and an elaborate mansion glittered in the distance, highlighted by the last rays of the sunset and the gathering twilight. Mark's mind zeroed in like a laser, all thoughts of romance forgotten as he took in the large number of cars parked out front. A temporary stage had been set up and floodlights blazed over the red, white, and blue banners strung everywhere.

"Wow. This place is spectacular. Who owns it?"

"Local power couple. Tim and Kim Rigsdale. He's some bigwig in technology and she's his trophy wife. They love all the glitz and glamour."

"Looks like it," Geneva said, her gaze narrowed on the festivities. "Looks like they're holding some sort of party too."

"Yeah. You want to go?"

"Are you kidding? I'm a reporter. I always want to go."

Mark parked his Jeep near the end of one long row of luxury cars and climbed out. He walked around to help Geneva from the car, but she was already out and met him near the front of the vehicle.

"Exactly how well do you know these people?" she asked him.

"Not that well." He took in the sea of white faces around them wondering where all these strangers came from. "They're also known as the town snobs. And I'm not exactly their kind of guy."

"Really?" she looked him up and down. "Why not?"

"Too dark." He took her hand and led her into the crowd. He wanted to keep a hold of her to make sure they weren't separated. That's the excuse he was going with anyway.

Asshole Sutton blabbered away up on stage and all these rich white folks seemed enthralled with his every word. Several bystanders gave Mark hostile glares as they weaved through the crowd and he'd never felt more out of place in his life. Still, he'd promised Geneva a look around and that's what he intended to give her.

They skirted the perimeter of the rally, checked out the mansion in the distance, then eased into the crowd to see the candidate in action.

"Yeah," Geneva said, once they stopped near the middle of the throng. "Neither of us exactly matches their color palette, huh?"

"Rainbows are beautiful, baby." Mark winked at her then took another look around. He only recognized one or two people making him question how many attendees were from out of town. Being around all these creeps made his skin crawl and his hackles rise. "You ready to go?"

"Not yet." She pulled out her small digital recorder. "I want to see if I can get some sound bites from the attendees. Readers eat up all this political crap."

Mark let her go, crossing his arms and frowning as she approached a redneck-looking guy with a stained T-Shirt that read Sutton is God stretched over his enormous beer belly. Geneva tapped the man on the shoulder and he turned toward her, giving her a lascivious head-to-toe appraisal.

"Hello, sir," Geneva said. "I'm a reporter from the National Tribune and I'd love to get your perspective on Frank Sutton's campaign."

"And I'd love to get in your pants, baby."

"That's enough." Mark stepped forward and pulled Geneva aside. "We're leaving."

"No."

"Take your hands off her, boy," the redneck said. "Don't you have some liquor store to rob or cops to shoot?"

Livid, Mark clenched his fists to keep from laying the dude out flat and leaned in until he was nose-to-nose with the guy. "What did you say to me?"

"He said back the fuck off, boy." This from another man—white, mid-forties and dressed as if he walked off some Ralph Lauren ad; well, unless you counted the handgun prominently holstered at the waist of his khaki shorts. "We don't need your kind around here. And we always protect our own. Now unless you and your girlfriend here," he gave Geneva a disparaging glance, "want to start some trouble I can guarantee you won't survive long enough to finish, I suggest you get the hell off this property, boy."

"C'mon, Mark." Geneva tugged at his arm. Her hands shook as the crowds around them drew in closer, hatred and anger glittering in their eyes. "Let's go."

Nostrils flaring with rage, he glared at the redneck and Ralph Lauren dude. "C'mon."

As they walked away, people purposely jostled them or spat on their feet. A few even yelled out, "Go back to your own country, asshole!"

"This is my country," Mark snarled, despite knowing it was useless. These people didn't care about the fact he was born in America. They only cared about the color of his skin. But where did they all come from and why did Sutton think it was necessary to bring in strangers just to make him look good. Did he even know that these people weren't local?

By the time they got back to the Jeep, the rally had shifted from Sutton's bombastic speech to a full-blown party, with blaring rock music and shouts and cheers of "The American Way or No Way" from the audience.

Unsettled, Mark started his engine and took off back down the drive toward the highway without another glance back. Curving through the foothills up to the mansion, the incline hadn't seemed so steep, but it was much more noticeable on the ride down. Geneva sat beside him, oddly quiet.

"You okay?" he asked.

"Sure." She shook her head and frowned. "I guess I didn't realize there was still such racism prevalent around here."

"One more reason Frank Sutton is a prick."

She snorted. "True. I can see your point about that guy now. Won't be getting my vote."

"Then my job is done." Mark chuckled. "Where are you staying?"

"The Fireside Inn."

"Nice. I know the couple who own that bed and breakfast. Pretty cushy from what I hear." He eased around another curve, gaining a little speed. "Your newspaper goes all out, eh?"

"Well, like I said earlier, this is a big story for them." She shrugged. "If I can break it, they're hoping it'll go viral. Speaking of which, are you ever going to talk to me about those SEAL deaths?"

"That depends." His good mood had returned after leaving all those bigoted bastards behind and now he felt like teasing her a bit.

"On what?" She wrinkled her nose.

"On whether you agree to have dinner with me again tomorrow night." He hadn't exactly meant to ask her out again, but now that he had, damn if he could regret it. She was a nice diversion, and they both knew the rules. They were both using each other to get what they wanted. Geneva wanted her information; Mark wanted to keep her from getting it. What better diversion than a little physical attraction? Besides, he enjoyed being around her, when she wasn't pestering him about those suicides.

"Ah, I see." Her voice held a hint of amusement. "Blackmail."

"No, ma'am. No blackmail here." He raised a hand. "SEALs honor. I'll even sweeten the pot. You can spend another day with me and the crew. Ask us any questions you want, about my business, that is. Brothers In Arms."

"Your business, huh?" Geneva sat back in her seat and grinned. He could tell from the knowing sparkle in her eyes she was as into this cat and mouse game as he was. "How could I refuse then? Deal."

"Good." The headlights illuminated another, sharper curve in the road ahead and Mark eased down the brakes to slow the Jeep. Except when he pressed the pedal, nothing happened. He tried again, still nothing. Doing his best not to give in to his rising panic, he said, "Hold on."

"What?" Geneva asked. "Why?"

"Because I can't slow down."

She laughed. "Is that another pick-up line, because if so, it was really bad."

"Unfortunately, no." He stomped on the brakes now, doing his best to keep the Jeep steady as they barreled downhill. "The brakes aren't working."

Eyes wide, Geneva straightened and double-checked her seatbelt, then held firm to the door handle and the dashboard. "Seriously? What's wrong?"

"No idea." Mark scowled out the windshield. He'd just had the damned car in the week before for a tune-up and Jace had checked the brakes himself. All perfect. Those hostile stares and angry threats from the Sutton supporters back at the rally flew back to his mind. A sick tentacle of dread bored into his stomach. What was one more SEAL death when there'd been three already? If he was right and those suicides weren't suicides at all, then whoever was behind the deaths could be trying to kill him too. "Someone must've messed with them."

"Who would do that?" Geneva asked, her tone fearful.

Mark didn't answer, his gaze flicking over to her quickly before focusing on the treacherous road ahead. There was about five-hundred-feet of drive before they reached the highway and if he wanted to remain alive, he needed to get the Jeep stopped before they hit traffic. He glanced beside him and saw a sharp drop off. Pulling onto the berm wasn't an option.

Gravel crunched beneath the tires and pinged off the metal body of the car. Each time Mark stomped on the useless brakes there was a weird squeak then a hissing sound. Most likely fluid leaking against hot rotors. There had to be a way to get this thing stopped. Pulse pounding and sweat prickling under the collar of his polo shirt, Mark put his SEAL strategy skills to work, flicking on his high beams and squinting down the road in front of them.

About two-hundred feet ahead was a small, flat scenic pull-off area for visitors. It wasn't wide, but it was long, following the hillside overlooking the highway and ocean beyond. If he could swerve onto it and if he prayed hard enough, maybe they could slow down enough to not go over the edge. Honestly, it wasn't like he had a choice in the matter really. It was either the pull-off or careen headfirst onto the busy highway below and face certain death.

"What are we going to do?" Geneva said, her tone rising with hysteria. Her pale face glowed in the moonlight and her knuckles were white with the force of her grip on the dashboard.

"Shit!" Mark yanked on the parking brake, hoping to slow them down.

When that didn't work, he tried throwing the automatic transmission into D1 then D2.

Still nothing.

Heart in his throat he took a deep breath. "A vista's coming up. I'm going to veer onto it and hopefully get us slowed down. I need you to hang on for me okay, Geneva?"

Eyes wide and knuckles white, she gave a quick nod. "I'm hanging on."

"Good. Here we go." Mark did his best to keep his voice calm as he clutched the steering wheel tight and eased right. Losing his shit right now wouldn't help anyone. Courage wasn't the absence of fear. He'd learned that through years of commanding his unit in Kabul. Courage was acting cool and rational in spite of your fear.

The Jeep's tires hit the asphalt of the pull off and squealed loud. Heart racing about a million miles an hour, Mark jammed the brake pedal hard to the floor one last time and prayed for a miracle. Skidding sideways, time seemed to slow gradually in time with the vehicle, slowed, slowed, until they came to rest at the very edge of the pull off, halted in the end by a guardrail.

Stunned and shaken, Mark forced his tense muscles to relax and his lungs to fill with air. The night was silent around them, save for the call of an occasional bird and the low hum of the highway in the distance. He hazarded a glance over at Geneva to see her huddled in the corner, trembling.

Holy fuck, they were still alive. Alive and unharmed.

Without thinking, Mark reached over and undid Geneva's seatbelt then pulled her across the bench seat and into his lap, holding her close as she sniffled into the front of his shirt. Her warmth helped soothe his lingering anxiety and the smell of her shampoo—sweet, light and faintly citrus—reminded him of bright summer days and all that was good in life.

His adrenaline slowly burned away, leaving him shaken to his soul. His muscles felt too tight for his bones and his neck and shoulders ached from tension. Doing his best to hide his inner trembling, he took a deep breath and stared out across the landscape below. They could've been dead, could've been pulverized against the sharp rock faces, could've been…

Geneva raised her head and looked up at him, her cheeks wet with tears and her lovely hazel eyes glittering in the moonlight. Mark didn't think he'd ever seen anything more beautiful. She blinked several times before taking a deep, shaky breath. "Thank you."

"For what?"

"For saving my life." She clutched the front of his polo shirt tighter. "I don't think I've ever been so scared."

He let loose a relieved chuckle and pulled her close again because it felt so damned good. Her thudding pulse gradually resumed a nice steady rhythm against him and her warm breath tickled his skin through his open V-neck collar. "What about hanging off the building today? You seemed a little scared then too."

She buried her face against him. "Okay, yeah. Maybe then too."

"Right." Mark undid his own seatbelt and got out of the car before helping her down too. He fished his cell out of the back pocket of his jeans. "Let me call Jace and have him bring the tow truck to get this."

"He drives a wrecker too?"

"Like I said, he works part-time as a mechanic between classes at Brothers In Arms."

Mark held the phone to his ear, lacing the fingers of his free hand through Geneva's to maintain their much-needed connection. Man, oh man. If that Jeep hadn't stopped in the nick of time, they'd both be flattened on those jagged rocks below. He peeked over the edge of the cliff and shuddered.

"Burrell's Service and Towing, Jace speaking."

"It's Mark. I need you to come get me. Bring the truck."

"Dude, what happened?" Jace might talk like a typical So-Cal hipster, but get that guy on the battlefield and he could kick some serious ass. "Everything okay? You sound weird."

"We had a little accident with the Jeep. And yeah, we're fine." Mark relayed the evening's events in his usual brisk way. "How long?"

"I'm on my way. Fifteen-minutes max, if I floor it. Glad you and Geneva are okay, man."

"Me too. See you soon and be safe. Thanks, buddy."

Mark ended the call then led Geneva back toward the roadway and away from the cliff, they'd almost gone over. What they both needed right now was a way to forget about this horror show. Humor always seemed to help in tense situations, so he went for that. "Well, you can't say I'm a boring date."

"True." She stuck close to his side. "But I thought you said this wasn't a date."

"Do you want it to be a date?" he gave her some serious side-eye.

She shrugged. "I don't know. All I know is I really don't want to be alone right now."

"Yeah." He slipped his arm around her shoulders then leaned back against a nearby boulder. "Normal reaction after a near-death experience. Guys used to crowd into the mess hall and the officers' lounge after battles. No one wanted to get stuck inside their own heads after something like that."

"Exactly." She shivered in the chilled night breeze and he pulled her closer. "It's like every time I close my eyes, all I see is that guardrail coming at us and the terrifying sheer drop beyond."

"Well, it's over now and we're both okay." Mark dropped a quick kiss on the top of Geneva's head then squinted down at the highway. "Can't believe those bastards cut my brake lines."

"Are you sure it was deliberate and not just mechanical failure?"

"Jace serviced the Jeep last week. No problems at all. Those brakes going out was no accident."

She exhaled and leaned against him. "If that's true, then someone's targeting you."

His suspicions were more than confirmed on that subject, but he didn't want to get her all riled up again so he offered her an alternative theory. "Or it's a bunch of entitled assholes who think they can get away with whatever they want, like those guys from the rally." He shook his head and looked away. "Could go either way."

Headlights veered off onto the end of the drive and he snorted. "If that's Jace, then I'm pretty sure he broke the sound barrier getting here."

"No kidding." She peered around him to see down the road. "Looks like a tow truck to me. I think we're good."

"Yep." Mark smiled down at her. "We are."

Within minutes, Jace rumbled to a stop at their pull off and got out. "Man, you sure pick your spots for car trouble. That's a one-hundred-fifty-foot drop there, dude."

"Thanks for the reminder." Mark gave his buddy a flat look then walked over to the Jeep. "You back the tow truck into position and I'll direct you."

"Cool." Jace climbed behind the wheel once more and ten minutes later, they had Mark's car loaded up on the back of the flatbed and chained into position. "I'm telling you, man. There's no way those brakes went out on their own. I checked 'em myself last week."

"I know." Mark helped Geneva up into the cab of the truck then followed in behind her.

"Where to?" Jace asked.

"She's staying at the Fireside Inn," Mark said, tilting his head toward Geneva.

"Scoops, please," Geneva said. "My SUV's there and then I can give Mark a ride home."

Mark stared down at her and saw the spark of heat in her eyes, the hint of desperation in her expression, and recognized the same in himself. They both craved companionship and connection after what had happened. Neither of them wanted to be alone. "Yep. Scoops."

"Okay, then," Jace responded, that devilish twinkle back in his brown eyes. "Scoops it is."

CHAPTER NINE

"So, here we are." Geneva swerved up to the front of a quaint looking older farmhouse situated near the edge of the Brothers In Arms compound, close to a neighboring vineyard. From the wide porch wrapping around the place, to the intricate gingerbread-style fretwork decorating the exterior, it looked like something right off the set of a movie. "You live where you work? That's dedication."

"A SEALs work is never done." Mark winked then undid his seatbelt. "You want to come in?"

A sudden burst of nerves jolted through Geneva's system. Back at the accident scene, she'd been pumped full of adrenaline and primed to jump this gorgeous man's bones. Now, with the reality of spending the night with him staring her in the face, Geneva's old insecurities reared their ugly head. She wasn't exactly a one-night stand type of girl, but some good, old-fashioned cuddling sounded damned near irresistible right about now. She couldn't seem to shake the chill from her bones or the terror of those last seconds before Mark had stopped the Jeep from her mind. Decision made, Geneva cut the engine and flashed him a brief smile. "Sure. Yeah. I'll come in for a second."

They got out and walked up onto the porch. The wood creaked beneath her steps, but the place looked well-cared for, with fresh paint on the walls and lush potted plants hanging from the rafters above. Mark unlocked the door and walked inside first, flipping on the lights before inviting her in.

"Please excuse the mess." He gestured toward what she considered an immaculate room. Her tiny apartment back in San Francisco looked downright shabby compared to this. Not that she didn't keep it clean, but it was hard to create a home when she traveled so much for her job. Geneva wasn't complaining about her lack of roots. She loved what she did, but her career required certain sacrifices. Namely any kind of steady home or personal life.

"This place is gorgeous," she said, taking in the large open-concept great room and gleaming hardwood floors. "When was it built?"

"Eighteen-ninety-two." Mark tossed his keys onto a side table then walked through the living room and into a large country-style kitchen filled with fancy stainless steel appliances. "I did a lot of the modern restorations myself."

"Wow. A man of many talents." She moved to stand before a granite breakfast bar. "I'm impressed."

"Don't be. The guys helped a lot too." He opened the double refrigerator then glanced at her over his shoulder. "You want a beer?"

"Sure." Geneva did her best not to stare at his firm ass as he bent over to grab their drinks. It was unfair, him being so damned attractive. He reminded her of that action movie star—Dwayne Johnson—only hotter, if that were possible. Her knees tingled and her core clenched and she took a seat on one of the stools at the counter to avoid collapsing into a puddle of goo at his feet.

Remember why you're here, girl. Remember the story.

"What are you going to do about what happened tonight? Will you press charges?" she asked, hoping to get her mind out of the gutter where he was concerned and back on track with her story. "If those people would cut your brake lines, they could hurt someone else too."

He twisted the caps off two bottles of ale, handed her one, and then took a seat on the stool beside hers. "Doesn't seem much point in filing a police report yet, since Sutton seems to have all the local law enforcement in his pocket; at least right now. Besides, I don't have any proof, not until Jace fixes the jeep and gets a look at the brakes. Besides, it was my fault for letting down my guard around them. I shouldn't have taken you there in the first place."

She shrugged, and assessed his defensive posture from over the rim of her bottle as she took a drink—all stiff shoulders and narrowed gaze. Obviously, this wasn't a subject that was up for discussion right now. She tried a different angle instead. "You

80

and your business partners seem really close. You all served together?"

"Three tours." Mark took a long swig of his ale. "Why?"

"No reason. Just trying to make small talk." She set her beer aside and wandered over to one wall in the living room covered with photos. Some were of Mark and the guys, some were of Mark and Leila, some were of Mark and an older Polynesian woman Geneva assumed was his mom. "Tell me more about Brothers In Arms."

"What do you want to know?" He finished off his beer before joining her, the heat of his body penetrating her thin cotton top and making her yearn with unexpected need. The accident must've affected her more than she thought. This close, he smelled of salt and sea and sandalwood cologne and Geneva had the crazy urge to bury her face in his strong chest and inhale deep. Instead, she took a step away and stared at more photos— these looked like construction pictures of their facilities. "How much land do you guys own?"

"Forty acres."

"That's a lot in these parts."

"We need it." He moved toward her and she moved away. "For all the different types of training classes we conduct."

"Right." Geneva swallowed hard, her heart rate quickening as her gaze flicked to his full lips. Would they feel as soft as they looked? She forced words past her suddenly constricted vocal cords. "Is all the property grassland?"

"Some of it. Our holdings extend to the foothills on the one side, with some flatland access too. The other side leads down to a small cove with a rocky beach. Gives us a lot of options with our classes."

"That's, uh, that's great." Geneva inched to the side and realized she'd backed herself right into a corner. *Smooth move, dumbass.* Her reporter instincts told her to go in for the kill, to ask him bluntly about his feelings toward the military's cutbacks on mental health spending. That would surely get him out of his amorous mood and back into suspicious business mode.

The rest of her, though, demanded she sink into him, let go and let whatever happened between them happen, find out if all those rumors were true about men with big hands and feet, because damn, his were huge.

"Are you from Ortega originally?" Her words emerged as little more than a whisper.

"Born and raised." He moved closer still, the heat of him enveloping her as he leaned one forearm against the wall beside her head. With only inches separating them now, his minty, alcohol-laced breath ghosted across her cheeks and his muscled chest brushed against her hard nipples. Geneva bit her lip to stifle a moan. It had been so long since she'd been with a man, what with her crazy schedule and ruthless work ethic.

Her body felt hot, starved and wanton. Without realizing what she was doing, Geneva arched her back to keep her body in contact with his. Mark's answering deep chuckle and knowing gaze sent a sizzle of molten heat straight between her legs. He shifted slightly and leaned in farther to nuzzle the sensitive spot on the side of her neck, just below her ear. His voice all but purred against her skin. "You don't really want to talk about my past, do you?"

Hell, no.

Hands shaking, Geneva slid her fingers up his beefy arms and around his neck, twining them around the nape of his neck. He shuddered against her at the gentle touch and she was lost. Lost to the moment and lost in him. Before she could stop him, Mark had pulled away and stared down at her, his expression serious.

"We've both been through a lot tonight, Geneva," Mark said, his breathing rapid. "I don't want to do something we'll regret later, no matter how good it feels now. I've got a guest room upstairs you're welcome to use, if you want."

Touched by his gesture, Geneva blinked up at him. His hard cock pressed against her soft lower belly and his pupils were blown wide, nearly obliterating his gray-green irises. All the physical signs said he was just as turned on as she was, yet still he behaved like a gentleman. That only made Geneva want him all the more.

To eliminate even the shadow of a doubt from his mind, she slid one of her hands down Mark's chest to the front of his jeans and stroked the hard length of his manhood through the soft denim of his jeans. Mark inhaled sharply and leaned his head back, eyes closed and expression full of pleasure.

"What I want…" She kissed and licked the pulse point at the base of his neck exposed by the open collar of his shirt. He tasted salty and sweet and utterly addictive. "…is for you and me to forget all about what happened on that hillside and to affirm what's real and true and alive tonight. I want to be with you, Mark. Do you want to be with me?"

"Fuck yes!" He moved so fast, one-second Geneva was standing in the corner, her back pressed against the wall and her front pressed against him, and the next she was swept up into Mark's embrace, her arms going around his neck and her legs coiling around his waist. His lips and hands seemed to be everywhere on her at once as he carried her across the living room toward the carved wooden staircase.

"Let's do it then," Geneva said, giggling into the side of his neck at her unintended pun.

"Oh, we're going to do it all right, *manamea*."

"What does that mean?" she asked, in between nibbles on his throat. "That word?"

"Sweetheart," he said, pausing halfway up the stairs to kiss her deeply. He tasted of mint and beer and pure, decadent passion. "In Samoan."

They reached the top of the stairs and Mark pushed through the doorway at the end of the hall into his bedroom. Geneva couldn't ever remember being so turned on or so desperate for physical connection with someone in her life. She ignored the niggle deep in her gut that said this might be something more than a one-night stand and put it down to their near-death experience on the cliff. Best to enjoy her one night in paradise then move the hell on before she got hurt again.

Mark placed Geneva gently onto the center of his king-sized bed then followed her down, his wicked grin wide. She hastily tugged his polo shirt from his jeans and pulled it off over his head before doing the same with her top. Then she reached for her bra clasp, but he stopped her.

"Nope. I want to unwrap my own present, thanks. And believe me; I plan to take my time."

CHAPTER TEN

Mark kissed his way down Geneva's neck to her collarbone, loving the feel of her fingers stroking his hair, the scrape of her nails against his scalp. He hadn't been kidding when he said he would take his time. He planned to kiss and lick and otherwise adore every single inch of her before this night was through. He wasn't sure if it was the accident or the forbidden nature of their tryst—given their opposing objectives—but damn, he hadn't been this raring to go in a long, long time.

After removing her bra, he nuzzled the valley between her breasts, tracing his tongue up to one of her hard, pink nipples before taking it into his mouth and sucking gently. She groaned beneath him. Her skin felt like silk and tasted like strawberries and cream. She seemed so responsive to his every touch, so attuned to him in ways his previous lovers hadn't, that it worked on Mark like a powerful aphrodisiac. His hard cock pressed against the fly of his jeans, eager to play, but there was no rush. Nope. It had been far too long since he'd slept with a woman, and tonight was all about taking things slow and savoring each delicious moment. He moved to her other breast and treated it to the same lavish care before kissing a path slowly down her belly. He reached for the button on her waistband, but Geneva grabbed his hand.

"Wait," she said.

Damn. Disappointment swelled inside him. Mark closed his eyes and rested his forehead against the warm skin of her belly. He knew it was too good to be true. Things between them had been too perfect, too easy. If Geneva wanted him to stop, though, he would. No matter how much he wanted the feel of her in his arms, the taste of her arousal in his mouth, he'd never taken an unwilling woman to his bed and he wouldn't start now. Mark sighed, removing both hands from Geneva's body and holding them in the air as he sat up. "Okay. If you want to stop, we will."

"No. I don't want to stop. I just…" She rolled away from him then got out of bed. She pointed toward a door in the opposite wall. "Bathroom?"

He nodded.

"Be right back."

Mark watched her disappear into the other room and close the door. He flopped back onto the mattress, his knees hanging over the edge, and scrubbed a hand over his face. He was twenty-eight-fucking-years-old today. He'd had countless lovers in the past but still apparently had no clue about the inner workings of a woman's mind. He stared at the ceiling above for what felt like hours, but couldn't have been more than a few minutes until the bathroom door opened again. He leaned up on one elbow and his breath caught in his throat. Geneva stood clothed only in her panties and socks, bathed in the pale moonlight streaming in through his windows.

She tucked a long curl of her auburn hair behind her ear and moved closer, her gaze dropping shyly as she placed her jeans and boots on the floor. "So, yeah."

"Wow!" He stayed on the edge of the bed and took in the vision she presented, all soft skin and curves a man could lose himself in. His throat felt dry, his voice husky with need as he whispered, "Come here."

Geneva moved slowly to stand between his open legs. Gently, he placed his hands around her waist and rested his forehead against her bare stomach once more. "You are so beautiful."

"I'm not." She caressed her fingers over his shaved scalp and he couldn't suppress another shiver. It felt amazing when she touched him. "But thanks for saying so anyway."

"To me you are gorgeous." Mark kissed the delicate skin just above the waistline of Geneva's panties and she moaned. He moved a bit lower, to the front of her undies, and inhaled the spicy scent of her arousal before licking her folds softly through the material. With one hand, he nudged her legs a bit wider and licked her again, over and over until the material of her panties was drenched and her legs were shaking so bad he feared she'd fall to the ground if he let her go. Not that he planned to let her go any time soon.

Mark stood and picked Geneva up again, laying her back on the bed before reaching to remove her lacy thong. Eyes heavy with passion, she looked at him. "Promise me you'll leave the socks on, okay?"

"Mine or yours?" he joked, tugging her undies down her calves and ankles, past the fluffy pink socks on her feet. When she didn't laugh, however, he relented. Yeah, it was kind of strange and made him even more curious to see what was under there, but if the socks made Geneva feel better their first time together, fine with him. Her feet weren't the part he was anxious to get to anyway. "Okay. Promise. Socks stay on for now, but one of these days I'll kiss each and every one of your delectable little toes."

Geneva gave him an odd look as he slid down on the bed beside her. Mark turned to kiss her, but she ducked away. Frowning, he pulled back again. "What?"

"Nothing. I just..." Geneva shook her head then glanced back at him. "Nothing."

Before he knew it, she pulled him down for a hard, open-mouthed kiss and couldn't seem to keep her hands off his cock. Good thing he still had his jeans on or he might've embarrassed himself, he wanted her so damned bad.

He hated to rush this first time, but his body demanded more. There'd be time to take it slower later. From the way she was moaning and arching against him, Geneva seemed more than ready too.

Mark stood and stripped off his jeans in record time then grabbed a condom from the nightstand drawer beside his bed and put it on. God, all he could think of right now was being inside her. His hands shook as he climbed above her again then traced his fingers slowly down her skin until his hand rested between her parted legs. She was so hot and wet and ready. He parted her slick folds and circled her clit with his fingers.

"God, yes!" Geneva bucked hard, pressing her wet folds against his hand. "Right there."

He continued playing with her clit with his thumb while sliding two fingers inside her, preparing her for his body. Her pleasure only served to drive his own need higher, but Mark refused to take his pleasure until she'd climaxed at least once.

With his other hand, he toyed with her nipple while sucking on its twin. Soon, Geneva cried out and arched against him, her inner walls contracting around his fingers as she rode out her orgasm.

"That's it, *manamea*," he whispered against the side of her breast. "Give me your passion."

Moments later, she stilled beneath him and he positioned his cock at her wet entrance. Holding his weight above her with his elbows, Mark stared down into her half-lidded eyes. "Ready?"

"Yes," Geneva said, her tone sleepy and sated. "I want to feel you inside me."

He hissed in satisfaction as he entered her hilt deep then held still, allowing her body to accommodate to his. Her hands slid around his neck once more and she locked her feet behind his lower back. Mark moved slowly within her, his rhythm increasing gradually until they were both poised on the edge of climax. He reached in between them and stroked her clit, driving her over the brink.

"Oh, yes!" Geneva's head fell back as she lost herself in ecstasy again and Mark couldn't hold back any longer. He drove hard into her—once, twice, three times—before he came hard. The world around him shattered into a million iridescent shards and he hung his head, his forehead pressed to her chest as he rode out his climax.

Finally, relaxed and exhausted, he stretched out beside her then spooned Geneva to him, her back to his front before pulling up the covers. He was just starting to drift off when she wriggled out from under his arm. Squinting one eye open, Mark scowled across the room. "Where are you going?"

"You said there's a guest room, right?"

"Yeah, next door. But—"

"Hey, you said you liked openness, yeah?" She gathered up her clothes then headed for the door. "Well, here's me being open. I'm not looking to settle down. I'm here for a job and that's it, okay? This was nice, but now I need to sleep."

She was gone before he could answer.

With a sigh, Mark lay back against his pillows and rubbed his tired eyes. Lord help him. She was a puzzle, but there was something about Ms. Geneva Rios. Something beyond her snooping reporter ways and her weird socks-stay-on thing. Something that went far deeper. He was intrigued enough to want to find out exactly what it was, but given her current skittishness, he wasn't sure he'd ever have the chance.

CHAPTER ELEVEN

The next morning, Geneva rose before dawn and showered before putting on her clothes from the day before and sneaking downstairs, hoping to get out of Mark's house and back to her hotel before he was even awake.

Unfortunately, beating a former SEAL out of bed was harder than she'd anticipated. Her stockinged feet had barely hit the hardwood on the first floor when Mark called out from the kitchen. "Want some coffee?"

With a sigh, Geneva crossed the living room and took a seat on the same stool she'd sat the night before. Mark looked bright eyed and bushy tailed and far too sexy for this early in the morning. He slid a steaming mug across the breakfast bar to her and she mumbled her thanks before spooning in some sugar and topping it off with a dash of cream. Not surprisingly, Mark took his black.

"So," Geneva said, looking anywhere but at him. "Last night was...*nice*."

"That's one word for it." He watched her over the rim of his cup. "Sleep well?"

"Great, thanks."

Awkward silence descended as he took a seat beside her. Finally, Mark tapped his fingers on the granite bar top and nodded. "We're, uh, doing more classes today at Brothers In Arms, if you want to stop over."

"Same group I rappelled with?"

"Different one, I think." Mark took another sip of his coffee. "Jace and Vann are running things today while I catch up on stuff in the office. But I'll let them know you're coming to watch, if you want."

"Sounds great, thanks." She took another gulp of caffeine, and then checked her watch. "What time do they start?"

"Nine."

"I better get back to the B&B and get changed then, so I can be ready." She stood and smoothed her hand down the legs of her jeans then pulled the SUVs keys from her pocket, not wanting to rush out but not wanting to stay either. She needed time to process everything that had happened between them last night, not to mention small talk wasn't exactly her forte in the morning. "You need a ride or anything?"

"Considering I live here on the premises and my office is just across the parking lot I should be fine." He watched her with a narrowed gaze, a spark of passion in his smile. "Unless you have a different kind of ride in mind."

Right.

Heat prickled up from beneath the collar of her shirt and Geneva looked away fast from the wicked twinkle in his eye. Definitely time to go before she tackled him to the floor and ravished him all over again. "I'll see you later this morning."

"See you around." Mark raised a hand as she backed toward the door.

"I had a good time last night."

"Just good?" He chuckled. "I must be losing my touch."

Remembering his touch, bringing her to orgasm again and again, Geneva tripped over her own feet. She fumbled with the door handle and didn't dare look at Mark again as she scrambled outside with a muttered. "Bye."

At least by the time she drove back to the Fireside Inn, she felt a bit calmer. Her raging pulse had quieted and her hormones seemed back under control. She parked the SUV near the front door and walked into the lobby of the bed and breakfast that catered to mainly business people. This morning, however, a gaggle of people wearing press badges filled the serve-yourself breakfast nook. Curious, Geneva stopped by the registration desk before heading up to her room.

"What's going on?" she asked the clerk.

"Oh, they're in town to cover the big fundraiser this afternoon."

"What fundraiser?"

"For Frank Sutton. He's running for Congress."

"Right." She suppressed a shiver at the suspected sabotage to Mark's vehicle. Mark didn't seem to want to pursue it, but that didn't mean she couldn't do some nosing around on her own. And it might give her an opportunity to get a sound bite or two directly from the candidate himself before his redneck battalion of supporters showed up. "Is it open to the public?"

"Yep," the clerk said. "Downtown, center square, three p.m."

"Thanks." Geneva headed for the stairs. If she used her time wisely, she'd be able to hit both the classes at Brothers In Arms and the rally. Hopefully Sutton would have an opinion on the SEAL suicides she could use to beef up her article. Given Mark had told her Sutton was an ex-SEAL himself, maybe the congressman wannabe could give her some fresh insight on the whole issue.

Two hours later, after a change of clothes and some breakfast, Geneva felt revitalized. She drove back through Ortega and saw firsthand the preparations for the upcoming fundraiser. From the size of the area blocked off and the number of banners and signs, it looked like they were expecting quite a crowd. She turned off the main drag and headed toward the outskirts of town and the Brothers In Arms compound. It was now a little after nine and the sun was shining. A good day for training, given the types of situations and terrain the guys said they prepared their clients for. You could never plan when or where you might be attacked and a lot of companies did business in areas where all sorts of nefarious behavior and unrest were prevalent.

Images of the previous night—the terrifying moments before Mark brought the Jeep to a stop, the comfort she'd felt in his arms afterward, the passion they'd shared in the dark hours following—flooded Geneva's mind before she shoved them aside. Time to work, not daydream about things that would never amount to more than a brief fling.

The class had already started by the time Geneva parked her SUV beside the company's Humvee. She climbed out and stood for a moment, one hand over her eyes to block the glare of the sunlight as she watched about twelve men of varying ages grapple with each other on mats spread out over a large field.

"Glad you made it back," Mark said, coming out of the nearby office building and striding over to her. "The guys are working on self-defense today. How to escape. The best tactics to employ when running away to increase your chances of staying free and alive."

"Huh." Several of the students attempted what looked to her like a standard foot swipe without much success. "Seeing how inept your current batch of students is, looks like they'd all be dead in less than thirty seconds."

"The point isn't to be tough. The point is to survive. And the best way to stay out of trouble is to avoid it in the first place." Mark gave Geneva a look. "Are you always this cynical?"

"Are you always such a boy scout?"

"Whatever." He sighed then pointed toward some bleachers along one side of the field. "Watch for as long as you want from over there. I'd join you, but I've got a conference call with a potential new client in five minutes. You want to grab some dinner again tonight?"

"Um, sure." Geneva shrugged. She didn't have any other plans and he was just about the only person she knew in town. Plus, the possibility of another night in his bed and the chance to probe his past some more didn't hurt either. "What time?"

"Around seven? I can pick you up at the Fireside. Jace said he'll have my Jeep fixed by then."

"Sounds good." She started to back away, remembering the fundraiser later. "Don't worry about picking me up, though. After I leave here, I've got a couple of other stops to make then I need to get some work done back in my room. I'll meet you back here."

"Okay."

"Okay." She grinned and waved. Truthfully, Mark could've picked her up, but him coming to get her would've been too much like a date and Geneva wanted to avoid any appearance of that at all costs. This was all about the sex, not romance. She climbed up the creaky wooden bleachers and took a seat on the top row to watch the action.

By around two that afternoon, Geneva had seen Jace and Vann put the guys through what she thought of as a basic self-defense course taught at any YMCA, with maybe a few special SEAL-esque tricks mixed in for fun. She took notes of what she observed on her tablet computer, along with a few short video clips, and then stored it all away for later. Right now, she had a fundraiser to crash. The accident last night had gotten her riled and she intended to see just how involved this Frank Sutton and his supporters might be, even if Mark seemed more content to forget about the whole thing.

She stood and waved to Jace and Vann. Jace waved back. Vann just stared at her. Typical. Then Geneva headed back to her vehicle. She had to say that Mark's apparent pacifist tendencies where last night's attack were concerned surprised her, given his military background, but Geneva had no problem going after the guilty party. Hell, given the career she'd like to build for herself as an advocate for those without a voice or representation, one might even say persecuting those in power was her life's mission.

Starting the SUV's engine, Geneva cranked the AC, pulled out of the parking lot and headed back toward downtown Ortega. Already, the streets of the tiny town were congested with traffic and probably the entire police department was out in force, directing cars and corralling visitors for the fundraiser.

It took her twenty minutes to find a place to park, and then she had to walk five blocks to return to the town square. Just as it had been the night before at the mansion, the attendees were predominately white and male and there was a general air of tension and anger permeating the air. A part of her wondered where everyone came from since Santa Barbara county wasn't exactly known for housing white supremacists. Oh sure, there were a fair share of most any marginal group everywhere, but this seemed like way too many for such a bedroom community. The number of buses she'd passed as she walked were an easy answer but she couldn't resist her curiosity.

Geneva kept to the fringes of the crowd, hoping to snag some one-on-one time with Frank Sutton before his speech. She made her way toward the makeshift stage set-up toward the front of the area and spotted the candidate himself near the sidelines, talking with a white couple who looked to be in their early forties and quite affluent, based on their hipster designer clothes. Geneva inched nearer to Frank Sutton and not so accidentally bumped into him. The couple Sutton was with looked at Geneva with the same level of disdain that most people reserved for dog poo on the bottom of their shoe. She ignored their hateful stares and flashed her brightest smile instead. "Oh. I'm so sorry."

"No problem," Sutton said. He looked her up and down then gave her the same fake plastic smile every politician must learn before they hit the campaign trail. "Frank Sutton. Running for Congress."

"Geneva Rios. Reporter for the National Tribune."

"National Tribune, eh?" The interest level in Frank's expression increased. "I'd love to be featured in their paper. Coast-to-coast syndication, right?"

"They don't call us National for nothing," Geneva said, giving him a wink.

"Are you here to cover my campaign?"

"Not exactly, but I did have a few questions for you, Mr. Sutton."

"Anything for my friends in the press." He put his arm around Geneva's shoulders and pulled her in tight for a squeeze while a cameraman took their photo. "Need to get more Latino voters on my side. Ask away."

"You're an ex-Navy SEAL, is that correct?"

"I am." His chest practically puffed with pride. "A true American hero."

"Frank," the rich white woman from the couple she'd seen earlier pushed in beside Geneva. "We really need to finish our conversation."

"Just a minute, Kim," Frank said, his attention still focused on Geneva. "I'm busy with an interview."

Kim gave Geneva a disdainful stare before turning back to her husband.

"Have you met my biggest supporters yet, Geneva?" Frank asked, apparently oblivious to the sour expressions of the couple. "May I introduce Tim and Kim Rigsdale. They donated more money than anyone else to my campaign. Geneva here is a reporter for the National Tribune."

So these were the owners of the mansion.

The Rigsdales each gave her a limp noodle handshake.

"What kind of distribution rates does your paper have?" Kim asked, looking down her nose at Geneva.

"Like the name implies, we're nationally distributed."

"Yes, but we're only interested in New York Times or Washington Post sized numbers," Tim said, forming a veritable white-skinned wall by standing shoulder to shoulder with his wife. "It's all about the fundraising. If you can't produce that kind of money for us, then any interviews with you aren't worth our candidate's valuable time. You understand."

Yeah, Geneva understood all right.

Asshats.

"Oh, and here's Kevin Quinn." Frank waved over another white guy, with dark hair and eyes and a non-descript suit. "Kevin, this is Geneva Rios. She's a reporter for the National Tribune and wants to interview me. Kevin here is an ex-SEAL too."

"Ortega's just crawling with you guys, huh?" Geneva smiled as she shook the guy's hand firmly.

"Nice to meet you," Kevin said.

"Kevin," Kim Rigsdale called. "We need you, please."

"Excuse me," Kevin said, giving Geneva the first genuine smile she'd seen around this fundraiser. "It was great talking with you."

"You too," Geneva said before turning back to Frank and taking out her digital recorder. "Is it okay if I record this, Mr. Sutton? My main purpose in coming here was to find out more about the recent rash of suicides among ex-Navy SEALs. I'm investigating how the military handles reintroducing vets back into society after times of war and how our current VA system is failing these guys."

"Now you're in my territory, Ms. Rios," Frank said. "I'm always looking out for another great cause to support and I'm glad you're trying to bring this story to light."

"Specifically, Mr. Sutton, I'd like to get your opinion on the recent rash of SEAL suicides in this area. Two good men recently killed themselves because they didn't get the support they needed from the military. In my research, I discovered their mental health benefits through the VA had been cut drastically over the last two years. The current plans before Congress now would cut those already-reduced benefits even more. How do you plan to address this if you're elected, Mr. Sutton?"

"Oh, well." Sutton glanced around, as if looking for back up, but none was forthcoming. "Our veterans are a national treasure, Miss Rios, and I have a comprehensive plan to help them as much as possible."

"Perfect." Geneva narrowed her gaze. "What exactly do you plan to do?"

Sutton blinked several times then checked his watch. "My goodness, look at the time. I need to prepare for my upcoming speech. I do hope you'll be able to feature our talk in your little newspaper. Do you think there might be a way to spin it so I could get some good campaign coverage out of it as well? Maybe work my name into the headline or something?"

Geneva gave him a blank look. Sutton seemed crazy as hell, but harmless enough. His supporters though? Well, that remained to be seen.

"Do you want to make an official statement on the suicides, Mr. Sutton?" Geneva tried to get the conversation on track. "That way I could include it in my article."

"Well, other than I'm glad you're shedding light on the incidents and what needs to be done to help these men, I can't think of anything."

"Frank," Kevin Quinn called. "I'm sorry, but we really need to talk to you a moment before you go on stage."

"Right." Frank patted Geneva on the shoulder then started toward the stage. "Thanks again for coming, Ms. Rios. Vote Sutton for Congress!"

Frustrated, Geneva moved to the sidelines once more to watch the rest of the speech. As she expected, not a lot of substance, just the same old empty promises and rhetoric designed to appeal to blue-collar white America while ignoring any people of color or minorities. Still, it was weird he'd dodged her question about his plans for veterans benefits completely. Most politicians she knew couldn't wait to blab on endlessly about their brilliant ideas to fix the perceived wrongs of America.

Disheartened, she tuned out after the first five minutes and instead focused on the crowds gathered. Perhaps she could try to interview some of these supporters again. The crowd today seemed a lot more organized as though this wasn't their first time and maybe it wasn't for some of the attendees. There were lots of cheers and shouts and angry posturing and the pounding country rock music blaring from the speakers was nearly deafening. Still, recorder in hand, she approached a nearby group of men dressed in dress shirts and ties. "Excuse me, gentlemen. My name's Geneva Rios and I'm a reporter with the National Tribune. If you don't mind I'd like to ask you a few questions for a piece I'm doing about Frank Sutton and record your answers for my interview."

The first guy, mid-thirties with dark hair and pale skin, looked at her, his black eyes cold. He was wearing different clothes today, but his attitude reminded her of the preppy-guy from the night before. Was it the same person? "Why would I want to talk to you? Mr. Sutton says the media is biased and rigged against him. When he gets elected, all of you amoral, lying pieces of shit will get what's coming to you. Maybe sooner, if you don't watch yourself, bitch."

Stunned by the underlying current of violence in the man's tone, Geneva stepped back, her hands shaking hard enough that she dropped her recorder. She bent to pick it up and someone slammed hard into her side, knocking her to the ground. Bodies seemed to press in closer, closer, and her oxygen supply dwindled. She fumbled for her recorder and a heavy foot crushed her hand into the ground causing her to cry out in pain. Her mind kept looping the preppy guy's ominous warning:

You amoral, lying pieces of shit will get what's coming to you...

Get what's coming to you... Get what's coming to you...

It was almost as if the lyrics to the song and the cheers of the crowds had morphed into that same message. Dread and desperation clawed through her. She needed to get out of here.

Now.

No one offered to help her up, though several bystanders sneered down at her.

Eventually, Geneva managed to grab her recorder and climbed to her feet, cradling her sore hand against her chest as she plowed through the crowds to the edge of the area. What had just occurred left little doubt in her mind these seething people were more than capable of cutting Mark's brake lines or worse. She suddenly couldn't wait to get out of there.

Weaving her way through the police officers around the perimeter, Geneva headed back to her SUV then to the bed and breakfast, looking forward to a few hours alone to gather her thoughts and calm her emotions before she saw Mark again. How sad her country had become so divided over something as stupid as the color of someone's skin or their ethnic background. These old battles should've been settled long ago, yet still seemed to raise their ugly heads every four years when it came time to elect new government officials.

Very sad indeed.

Chapter Twelve

Mark finished his third conference call of the day and sat back with a satisfied smile. He'd managed to sign two more important, high-profile clients already today and this third one seemed like a good bet as well. Things were going well for Brothers In Arms. Going well for him personally too, considering his night with Geneva. The chemistry between them and the way she responded to his every touch was amazing. Hell, if he didn't know better, he'd think they were meant to be together.

Inhaling deep, he sat forward again. Except he did know better.

Frowning, he shuffled the papers on his desk. The sooner he remembered that and focused on what he needed to do—keep an eye on Geneva and what she was writing about while she was here; continue to investigate the murder/suicides of his friends; figure out who the hell had cut his brake lines the other night— the better off he'd be.

He and Geneva were fuck buddies during her stay in Ortega, nothing more. She'd made that clear last night when she'd left the comfort of his arms to sleep alone in the guest bedroom. No matter how compatible they might be in the sack. Mark finished up the contracts he'd filled out for the new clients, then closed the documents on his computer and opened his work email.

There at the top of the queue was a daily digest newsletter from the National Tribune.

Clicking it open, Mark flicked through the articles on his screen. Updates from the wars in the Middle East and northern Africa, today's weather, stock reports, and horoscopes. Near the bottom was the special interest section. He glanced at the top headline in the box then did a double take.

Top Private Security-Training Firm Brothers In Arms—Help or Hoax?

What the actual fuck?

The article, dated two days prior to when he'd first seen Geneva in the parking lot at Scoops, read like a copy and paste smear campaign of every false rumor and bad review on the Internet. It called into question his hiring practices for having taken on two recent employees who later committed suicide, then linked that to Geneva's stated agenda regarding the military's disregard for the mental health of its soldiers. The article even managed to tie things in with the death of Geneva's own brother, Jaime. By the time he'd finished the article, Mark was seething.

Where was the other side of the story, the true side of the story?

His company was expected to top one million dollars in profit that year and Mark made sure they donated to charity appropriately for their blessings. Where the hell was that information in that snide little article, huh? Where was the fact he and the guys routinely volunteered for Habitat for Humanity and at the local children's hospital? Nowhere, that's where. Because this article wasn't about doing good or seeing good in others.

This article was to sell papers. Period.

"Shit." Feeling pissed and betrayed, Mark shut down his laptop then charged out of his office to walk the perimeter of the grounds. This. This was exactly why he'd known better than to trust Geneva or her fucking trash bin of a newspaper. This was why he'd kept her at arm's length and not allowed her to get too close. Two days they'd known each other and she'd not said one word, not one, about this article or the awful things her paper had accused his company of.

He stalked across the now empty training field and headed for the flatlands. Whenever his emotions threatened to overtake him and he had shit he needed to work out, physical exercise always helped. And man, oh man, was he furious right now.

It felt like living with his father all over again.

Every smile, every look, every word out of Geneva's goddamned mouth was a lie.

Not that he'd trusted her completely, but Jesus. They'd fucking slept together last night. They'd almost fucking died together. Would it have killed her to admit her newspaper had published that nasty little article about his business?

Mark veered off from the flat, sunbaked trail he was on and headed toward the ocean cliffs instead. The sex had been good too, so damned good, and helped him forget for a while all the other shit going on in his life—the deaths he was investigating, the loan payments on the compound land that were coming due in a few months, the fact his mom wasn't getting any younger and would soon need more help at her restaurant.

Why couldn't Geneva have just stayed a nice, harmless little distraction?

Why did she have to go and betray him, just like he'd feared she would?

The fact the article had come out before she'd met him hovered around the edges of his mind, but he was too pissed right now to consider it.

Exhaling loudly, he stood at the top of the cliff that led down to the small cove owned by the company. This line of thinking was getting him nowhere, yet he couldn't seem to break himself out of the vicious cycle.

Below him, the ocean waves crashed against the shore and beckoned him closer. What he'd love to do was grab his board, change his clothes and spend the next few hours surfing away his tension and anger. What his responsibilities required, however, was that he head back to work and conduct business as usual. After taking one last, fortifying breath of salt air, he headed to his office, his thoughts still as tangled as his emotions.

Didn't help either when Vann interrupted his never-ending paperwork with the background check Mark had known he'd run on Geneva. So, now he knew that not only did she not tell him about the article, she'd failed to tell him about her personal connection to the suicide story too. Worst of all, was the fact he couldn't get the goddamned night they'd spent together out of his traitorous head. In fact, she'd been foremost in his thoughts all day. The way she'd tasted, the way she'd smelled, the way she'd refused to take off those stupid socks or sleep in his bed...

Geneva had lied. Lies of omission, yes, but lies all the same.

There was nothing Mark hated more than lies.

By the time Geneva arrived later that evening, he was livid. For a man who prided himself on never losing his cool, his lying little reporter had managed to accomplish the near impossible.

He sat behind his desk, waiting for her when she pulled into the lot. Tonight, they'd be doing a whole lot more than grabbing dinner. They'd be facing all this shit head on, once and for all. No more lies.

"Hey." Geneva walked in. She'd changed from earlier, he noted, from her jeans and basic white T-shirt, to a black mini-skirt and a fitted pink top. Still had on those same damned boots though. Another reminder of the secrets she was keeping. His indignation rose while she smiled sweetly as if nothing was wrong. "Hope I'm not late."

Mark remained seated and forced himself to take a deep, calming breath. "Got something you'd like to tell me?"

"About what?" Geneva stepped closer and tossed her bag onto one of the chairs in front of his desk. She winced slightly and rubbed her right hand. "You look tired."

"I am tired." He frowned. "Tired of all your shit."

"Excuse me?"

"You heard me." He scowled. "Why don't you tell me why you're really here, Miss Rios?"

"You know why I'm here." Geneva crossed her arms and met his gaze direct. "I'm investigating the rash of SEAL suicides."

"Why?"

"What do you mean why?"

"I mean why do you care about these men's deaths?" Mark pushed to his feet and came around the desk toward her. "Why come to my business about them, huh? Cut the crap, Geneva. I saw the awful little smear article in your paper about Brothers In Arms."

"What? I haven't written anything."

Flipping his laptop open, he pulled up the article and spun the machine around for her. Geneva sat down to scan the article. Fairly quickly, she began to shake her head.

"I had nothing to do with this. It must have been my boss who put the article together as a precursor to what I hoped to write."

Mark gritted his teeth. "Then why is your name on it?"

"He must have named me as a contributor because he included the story of my brother, which I'm not thrilled about but I didn't do this." She looked away. "Listen, I—"

"Show me what else you're writing."

"What? Hell, no." Crimson flushed her cheeks and her hazel eyes sparkled with fury. "See, there's this thing called Constitutional rights and freedom of the press."

"Right." A small muscle ticked near his clenched jaw. "So you *are* going to print a bunch more crap about us then?"

"I didn't say that."

"You didn't have to." His voice grew louder. "What about your brother?"

The color in her cheeks drained away. "What about him?"

"Were you planning on mentioning Jaime at some point?" Mark all but spat the words out, too pissed now to care. "Oh, wait. That would be a conflict of interest, huh? Wouldn't want your second-rate newspaper to get sued. Again."

"My brother has nothing to do with this."

"Funny, because I think your brother has *everything* to do with this. Sounds like Jaime came home, couldn't cope, and killed himself. Now, there's a bunch of other guys with the same problems and you can't help but project your brother's issues onto them and the whole military establishment. Sorry, lady. Conspiracies and lies are not my thing. This is exactly why I never should've had anything to do with you in the first place."

Expression furious, Geneva jabbed her index finger into Mark's chest. "First, my family's business is private. Second, what happened with my brother *was* the Army's fault. They failed Jaime. They let him come home without any resources, any treatment, not even a thank you for your service before they kicked him out on the streets to fend for himself. So, yeah. I've got a problem with that. I made a promise to my brother, the day I buried him, that I would bring this story to national awareness and I won't fail him twice. And if that means exposing the military's poisonous mentality and corrupt attitude then so be it."

"Poisonous mentality?" Mark tone turned jagged as shattered glass. "What the fuck are you talking about? I gave eight years of my life in service to my country. What the hell have you ever done? Our military should be praised."

"Sure. They train the paranoid to be more paranoid, right? What's not to praise."

"Why, you…" Mark stalked to the other side of the room. He needed to get some space before he smashed his fist through the wall, Hulk-style. He'd never met a more misguided, misinformed, maddening woman in his life. Unfortunately, his blood was also pumping and his adrenaline flowed hot through his veins, and fuck all if he wasn't more turned on than he could ever remember being in his whole goddamned life.

Jesus.

Furious at himself and frustrated beyond belief, Mark rubbed his hand over his head and kicked the toe of his boot into the baseboard, hoping to ease some of the unbearable tightness in his body.

"What's the matter?" Geneva taunted him from her spot in the middle of the room. "You talk a good game about being open and honest, Mark Rogers, but you can't take it in return?"

He shook his head, but kept his mouth closed, his hands clenched at his sides. "Excuse me?"

"C'mon," she continued, either not knowing or not caring how close he was to the edge, how bad he wanted to fuck her so hard and so long, until they both forgot about this stupid fight, all her stupid lies, and just connected physically again, like they had the night before. "What do you want, huh? Honesty or honey lies?"

"What do I want?" Acting on pure impulse, Mark strode over to Geneva, and then stopped himself. His fists were clenched at his sides and his breathing ragged. "Fuck!" He turned away. "I'm so goddamned torn right now I don't know what I want anymore."

After several tense moments, Geneva took a deep breath. "I'm sorry. I shouldn't have said those things about the military. It's not our troops that are broken; it's the system behind them. But I had nothing to do with the article and I'm upset about it too."

"I took you under my wing, showed you around my business, and shared parts of my life with you. I thought I could trust you," he managed to say past his constricted vocal cords.

"You can trust me, Mark." Geneva walked to his side, though she didn't touch him. "That article was not my doing. If I'd known he was going to write something like that, I would have insisted on being a part of it so the truth would come out; particularly once I got to know your family, your friends, and the kind of business you run."

Mark scrubbed a hand over his face then glanced over at her, his anger replaced now by resignation. "I might have overreacted a tad." He gave her a small half-smile. "I've been told I do that sometimes."

"No!" she said, placing a hand over her heart in mock horror.

"Yeah." He faced her now and reached out to run his fingers down her soft cheek. "Sorry."

"Me too." She caught his hand and brought it to her mouth, kissing each of his knuckles before sucking the tip of his index finger into her mouth. She watched him through narrowed eyes, licking his skin before releasing the digit with an audible *pop*. Her cheeks were flushed and her gaze sparkled with arousal. If Mark didn't know better, he'd think she was as turned on as he was. "Want to make it up to me?"

Seems he wasn't the only one whose fury had quickly transformed into sexual fire.

"I thought you'd never ask." He picked her up fast, ignoring her startled squeak of laughter, and then plunked her down on the edge of his desk. Several emotions flitted through her eyes at once—anger, challenge, passion, need. He kissed her hard and she dug her fingers into his scalp, scratching her nails hard against his skin, giving as good as she got. By the time he pulled back, they were both panting.

"I want you so damned bad, *manamea*." Mark tugged Geneva's shirt off over her head, then undid the front clasp on her bra before cupping her breasts in his hands. "This. This is what I want. I want to be inside you."

Mark kissed a path across her cheek to her earlobe, pausing to nibble on it before continuing down her neck to her collarbone. Geneva clung to him, gripping his shoulders tight as she arched hard against him. He tugged her closer, pushing up her short skirt and spreading her thighs so her panty-covered wetness pressed against his hard, aching cock through his jeans.

"I…want…," she said, her voice all breathy with need.

"What?" He bent and took one of her hard nipples into the warm wetness of his mouth before nuzzling the valley between her breasts. "Tell me what you want."

Geneva ground herself against him. "You. I want you."

Mark glanced over at the door, realized it was still unlocked, but damn if he could stop now. Besides, the prospect of someone walking in on them only added to the illicit excitement of their liaison. It was late, anyway. Classes had ended hours ago and Jace and Vann had headed home to their places in town. Now, only he and Geneva remained.

"Fuck yes, *manamea*." He shoved her skirt up to her waist and quickly tugged her panties down her legs then tossed them across the room before stroking his hands up her thighs and gently caressing her. Christ, she was so wet for him already.

As his thumb circled her hard clit, Geneva cried out. "Please, Mark…"

"Please what?"

"Please, fuck me."

She didn't have to ask him twice. Mark unbuttoned and unzipped his jeans, pulled a condom from his back pocket, then slicked it on before positioning himself at her wet entrance. He'd never taken a woman here in his office, but given the hotness of the situation and Geneva, it wouldn't be their last rendezvous here.

"Hold on tight," he said, before driving himself into her hilt deep. She groaned loud, locking her legs around his waist, her arms tight around his neck as he thrust into her over and over again, the rubber soles of her boots digging into the skin of his lower back with each thrust. Last night had been about a slow exploration of something new between them. Tonight was all about sex—hot, wet, rough, mind-blowing sex. Given the intensity of their passion, it didn't take long for Mark to feel that familiar tightening deep in his sac that signaled an impending climax.

"Are you close?" he growled, taking Geneva's earlobe between his teeth.

"Yes," she hissed, nuzzling the pulse point at the base of his neck. "So close."

"Good." Mark reached between them and stroked her clit, causing Geneva to clench her limbs around him tight. "Let go for me, *manamea*. Let go."

"Yes!" Her inner walls convulsed around his cock as she came hard. "Oh God, yes!"

He drove into her, his pace harder, faster, deeper now until his body stiffened and he climaxed within her. Throwing his head back, he shouted out her name as his orgasm shook him to his core.

Moments later, they clung to each other both panting and sweaty. He eased her back onto the edge of his desk and helped her straighten her clothes. "Are you okay?"

She nodded, not looking at him. "I'm good."

"Okay." Mark got his jeans buttoned and zipped then grabbed her panties from the floor. "Um, here."

"Thanks." Geneva snatched them from his hand then went behind his desk while he turned the other way to give her a bit of privacy. "Listen, about the article..." she said.

"I just wish I didn't have to find out about it on the Internet. If we're going to keep doing..." he gestured between them, "...*this*, then we need to be honest with each other on what we're working on. No more lies. Agreed?"

"Agreed." She came back to where he was standing, smoothing a hand down the front of her skirt. Her cheeks were still flushed with passion and her eyes had gone all dreamy and sated and it took all of Mark's willpower not to strip her down again and make love to her once more on the sofa against the far wall.

He eyed her and did his best not to let his old doubts take root in the present. "So you promise me you'll be honest with me from now on. About everything. Okay? That's all I ask. Just be honest."

"Okay." She grabbed her bag, rummaging through it as she said, "Here's me being honest. We can continue to have sex, but that's it. I can't let a relationship with you interfere with my purpose in being here."

"Which is Jaime."

"Yes." She looked over at him. "Always Jaime."

The words sucker punched him more than he expected. Mark wasn't dumb enough to think this was some sweeping love affair or anything more than two lonely souls looking for a bit of comfort. Still, his chest ached with unaccountable envy and he wondered what it would be like for her to feel the same loyalty for him that she felt for her deceased sibling. "Tell me about your brother."

She paused, glancing at him. "What do you want to know?"

"What kind of guy was he? Tell me the stuff I can't find on the Internet. Tell me about the real Jaime."

Geneva blinked several times, her expression going sad and wistful. "Jaime was the best brother ever. He was my best friend, my champion, my biggest supporter. He was always there for me when I needed a hug, a beer, or just an ear to listen." She leaned against the desk beside him. "All that changed though, after he came back from combat. Jaime was withdrawn, scared, wouldn't talk to anyone about what was happening with him. I tried to get him help, tried to work with the VA, but they just slammed the door in our faces. The day he died, a part of me died too."

Mark reached over and took her hand. "That's why you fight so hard for him."

"For him and all those out there who are suffering like he did." She sniffled and swiped the back of her free hands against her damp cheeks. "If I can save even one life by telling his story and uncovering the truth, then I have to do it. Can you understand that?"

He nodded, bringing their joined hands to his lips and kissing the back of hers, he noticed a few scratches and bruises on it and frowned. "What happened here?"

"Oh." She sniffed. "I stopped by that Sutton rally in town earlier. The crowds got a little out of hand and I dropped my recorder. When I went to pick it up, someone accidentally stepped on my hand."

Given his suspicions about who might've tampered with his vehicle, Mark doubted the injury was accidental, but he kept that to himself for now. This peace between them was nice, and most likely short-lived, given their penchant for disagreeing with each other. He wanted to enjoy the peace part for as long as he could.

Geneva remained silent for several moments before cocking her head toward the door. "Now are you going to feed me or what? I'm starving."

Mark gave her an incredulous look. "Seriously?"

Her stomach growled loud, as if in response.

"All right then." He let her go and grabbed his keys off the desk. "Food it is."

CHAPTER THIRTEEN

The next day, Mark was out in the training field on the Brothers In Arms compound, helping Jace and Vann double-check all of the obstacles they'd set up over the weekend for the new three-week-long classes starting that night. It was a new group of businessmen from one of his recently signed clients who'd requested not only security training, but a bit of Warrior Dash thrown in for fun.

They'd all been through similar courses during SEAL training, so putting it together had been a snap, especially with Jace's mechanical engineering abilities. As Mark climbed up the side of the framework for a barn-like obstacle called the Diesel Dome, he spotted Jace and Vann across the way inspecting what would become the mudslide once they added water to it. The point of the whole course was to test both the challengers' physical endurance and their fortitude. Given Mark was currently scaling a fifty-foot-high structure comprised of nothing but wood and air, they'd accomplished their goal.

He finished climbing to the top of the dome then stood to gaze out over the whole Brothers In Arms property. The view from up here was spectacular and with the slight breeze, he got a hint of the salty sea air drifting in from the Pacific in the distance. Maybe, once he was done here, he'd have time to hit the waves again. With business booming and everything going on with

Geneva, his surf time had been curtailed drastically over the past week and he missed it. Missed the time alone with just the ocean and his thoughts.

"You planning on taking a vacation up there or what?" Vann yelled to him. Apparently, he and Jace had finished up with the mudslide and were moving on to the Fisherman's Catch next—a series of nets strung across a ravine filled with muck and dirt. Challengers had to work their way across using skill and coordination or end up taking a bath in Lord knew what. Vann crossed his arms and raised a black brow at Mark. "We could use your help down here."

"Fine." Mark took one last deep breath of fresh air then stepped over onto the next board about three feet away. An ominous creak sounded from somewhere below, but he didn't hesitate. After all, Jace had put this stuff together with Vann's expert help, which meant it was nearly indestructible. "I'm coming. You guys need help with the class tonight?"

"Nah," Jace shouted from below. "It's only six students and— Oh, fuck! Mark, man, look out!"

Mark jumped to the next board and—an earsplitting crack filled his ears, the kind you'd expect from a huge oak branch sheering from its trunk.

Two realizations hit him at once.

First, he was fucked.

Second, there was nothing he could do to save himself.

"Oh shit!" The world tilted and he was in freefall. The last thing he remembered was the blue sky above and the brisk rush of wind on his face. Then a hard thud against his back. Pain shoved the breath from his lungs. Something knocked him hard on the head. A weird moaning echoed from somewhere and it took Mark a moment to realize the sound came from him. Blood pounded in his ears and his vision darkened at the periphery.

Fallen...I must've fallen...

Dazed and confused, Mark squinted up at a remaining patch of blue sky above as a cloud drifted over the sun. Shadows descended and the shouts of his buddies rang out around him. He tried to move his arms, his legs, tried to call out and answer them, but he couldn't seem to catch his breath. Trapped. He was trapped beneath what felt like six tons of shit. Agony radiated out from his temples as more wood rained down from above.

"Dude!" Jace shouted. "Mark, can you hear me?"

"Stay with us buddy," Vann called. "Help's on the way!"

Time lost all meaning as he lay there, every bone in his body aching. Eventually, another sinister creak sounded, followed by the distant wail of sirens then blackness as the rest of the Diesel Dome collapsed atop him. Unable to move, unable to breath, unable to do anything but lay there and stare up at the graying sky, Mark said a last silent prayer. For his sister, for his mom, for himself. This was it. He'd always imagined he'd die in combat or, if he was lucky, old age. Not like this. Never like this.

The sirens outside whined closer while Vann and Jace's panicked shouts grew more distant, until all became silent and still....

CHAPTER FOURTEEN

"Where is he?" Geneva asked as she burst into the waiting room at Ortega General Hospital. She spotted Jace and Vann sitting against the far wall of the emergency room waiting area and rushed over to them. "Is Mark okay?"

Vann gave her a cool stare, his voice flat. "He's having a CT Scan of his head now."

"Is he conscious?"

"Yeah, he's awake," Jace said. "Got knocked out though when he fell. He's pretty banged up and bruised too. Luckily, they don't think there's anything too seriously wrong though, as long as there's no traumatic brain injury."

Traumatic brain injury...

She sank down into a chair across from them and swallowed hard. When the call had come in across her police scanner about an accident with injuries at the Brothers In Arms compound, Geneva had feared the worst. Now, as the adrenaline in her system dissipated, she felt shaky and scared, her need to see Mark and assure herself he was okay all but obliterating any common sense she had left. "What happened?"

"That's what we're trying to figure out." Vann gave her another assessing look. "We built each of those obstacles ourselves, had them professionally inspected by local licensed contractors before any of us attempted to use them. This shouldn't have happened."

"No, it shouldn't." Jace raked a hand through his shaggy blond hair. "I can't help feeling it's my fault, man. Jesus, first Mark's brakes getting messed with and now this. I know what this looks like, but I swear it wasn't me. The guy's like my brother, man. I'd never do anything to hurt him. Never."

"No one thinks it's you." Vann clapped Jace on the shoulder then glanced at Geneva again, his expression shifting from concerned to hard in seconds. "Could have been someone else though. Someone with maybe an ax to grind against our business or the military."

Geneva frowned, her defenses rising fast against the accusation in his tone. "Me? I would never hurt Mark. Never. We're…" She managed to stop herself before blurting out that she and Mark were sleeping together, but just barely. Flustered and frazzled, Geneva pushed to her feet again to pace the length of the waiting room. "Look, I know you guys are leery of me because I'm a reporter, but you have to believe me when I say I would never hurt Mark. He and I are… working together on something." Vann gave her a flat look, his dark gaze far too knowing for her comfort. Still, what she and Mark were doing behind closed doors was no one's business. She shook her head and tried to focus on their current situation, using her well-honed reporter skills to piece the facts together. First Mark's car had been tampered with. Now the obstacle course. "You think it was sabotaged?"

"I don't think, I know," Vann said, his words granite tough. "The cops must suspect something too. They sent a team of forensic investigators to the site after the EMS got Mark from the rubble. I'll be assisting them once I leave here." Vann looked away. "Did some preliminary poking around too, before law enforcement arrived. Found some suspicious marks on some of the beams, like they'd been deliberately cut. And some footprints leading to and from the dome. Didn't match any of ours."

"Mark told me you're the best tracker he's ever met," Geneva said, staring down at her hands clenched tight in her lap. She replayed the night of the fundraiser, all those angry people. The Sutton rally downtown. His supporters seemed hell-bent on snagging the guy a congressional seat. The sneering disdain of the Rigsdales as they'd looked down their noses at her. Sutton's supporters seemed like a bunch of entitled, racist pigs, but would their hatred translate into murder? She shuddered. Wouldn't be the first time one person's beliefs, however twisted, resulted in violence and death for another person. "Do the police have any suspects?"

"Not yet." Jace sighed and stared down at the floor. "They're questioning our recent clients now." He sat back and rubbed his eyes. "Man, I just want Mark to be okay."

"We all do," Vann said, taking his seat again.

Shoulders slumped; Geneva joined them and picked up a well-worn copy of People magazine from a nearby table. The thing was four months old, but it didn't matter. She wasn't reading it anyway. All she saw when she looked at the pages was Mark's face that first day in the parking lot of Scoops, handsome as hell and full of snarky suspicion. Then later, when they'd driven up to the Rigsdale mansion. The feel of his warm, strong fingers entwined with hers. The way he'd guided her through those hostile crowds, so strong, so sure, so protective.

Warm pressure squeezed tight around her heart and Geneva frowned. When she'd made the choice to get involved with Mark beyond the professional, she'd promised herself it would stay totally physical, that she'd keep her emotions out of it. But now, it seemed, her emotions were riding roughshod over her vows to her brother. Somehow, someway, Mark had stormed right through her staunch barriers and found his way into her heart...

Then she'd had to go and mess it all up by repeating her stupid statement last night about it being only sex, about how she didn't want anything from him but his body. God, no wonder she was twenty-five and still single.

"Your friend is out of CT now," a nurse said from the waiting room doorway. "We've moved him into a regular room too. You can see him briefly, if you like."

"Thanks." Vann said, and then stood.

Jace pushed to his feet beside him. "You want to come in with us, Geneva?"

"Yes, please." Geneva hoped her wobbly knees would support her as she walked down the wide, brightly lit hall with the guys. She'd kept to herself a lot since Jaime's passing, always working, always staying busy, to avoid her grief. But connecting with these guys and being part of something again felt...*nice*. The white walls and tile floor gleamed beneath the florescent bulbs above. "Thanks."

"For what?" Vann asked, scowling.

"For letting me tag along."

Vann gave her a brusque nod in response while Jace grinned and winked.

They walked down the corridor, the rubber soles of her boots squeaking on the freshly waxed floor and the smell of antiseptic stinging her nose. She'd been in more hospitals than she could count after Jaime had his first breakdown. He'd been shuffled from one psych ward to another, given more drugs than she could count, yet nothing had helped with his depression and PTSD. She'd begged the VA to let him try some therapy, maybe get him into a rehab facility when the drinking became too much. But no. They'd refused to listen to any of her pleas.

"Hey, buddy," Vann said as he pushed into the last room on the right side of the hall. "You still with us?"

"Still here," Mark said from his hospital bed, his normally smooth voice tight with pain.

Geneva did her best not to look shocked at the stark white bandages swathing Mark's head or all the tubes and wires hanging from his gorgeous body. He was a young, healthy guy. He didn't belong in here. She wanted to run from the room and never come back. She wanted to run into his arms and never leave. Both things were unacceptable, so Geneva hovered just inside the door and did her best to blend into the background.

Mark, however, seemed to have other ideas. He caught her eye and Geneva moved close, as if drawn by some invisible cord that wrapped tight around her heart and tugged. "Does it hurt?"

"Nothing I can't handle. Not with the pain meds they've got me on anyway." Mark turned to Vann again. "Any idea what happened? That thing should've been solid as Mt. Everest."

"Let's see what the police find." Vann glanced over at Jace before continuing. "Can't say I'm surprised though, after what happened with your brakes. Oh, and I called your sister and mom. They should be stopping by later to see you too."

"Great." Mark frowned, his expression less than delighted. "Sutton's supporters roughed up Geneva too, at the rally downtown the other day," Mark said.

Geneva frowned. "What? No. I told you I dropped something and someone accidentally stepped on me."

Mark took her right hand and rubbed his thumb over the scrapes on the back. "I'm beginning to think with these people there are no accidents, *manamea*."

She swallowed hard and looked away. Damn if she wasn't feeling the same way. She hadn't told him just how threatened she'd felt that day at the rally, how she'd cowered on the ground with all those angry people towering above her, and she didn't intend to either. Mark had enough on his plate right now just getting better. She'd handle her suspicions about Sutton and his supporters her own way.

Jace exhaled loud and gripped Mark's bedrail tight. "I've been thinking about this a lot while we were in the waiting room. If someone tampered with the Diesel Dome, it would have to be someone familiar with engineering and technical specs to hide those cuts from me. Of course, they'd also have to be wily enough to sneak past our security and onto the grounds too."

"You're the best mechanical guy I've ever met," Mark said. "It would have to be a genius to get something past you, bud. Besides, we don't know anyone like that, do we?"

"We might," Jace said, meeting Mark's gaze.

"Who?" Vann asked, nose scrunched.

"Tim Rigsdale."

"The couple supporting Frank Sutton?" Geneva was stunned. Yes, they'd seemed snobby and far too rich for their own good, but hardly the kind of people to get their hands dirty. "I doubt it was them. They don't seem like the type. And Mark, I thought you said he was some tech mogul."

"He is." Mark shrugged, and then winced. "But Tim's original degree was in engineering."

Lowering her gaze, Geneva dug the toe of her boot into the tile floor. "The other day, at the rally, Sutton introduced me to them. They weren't exactly overjoyed to meet me, given my ethnic heritage, but they hardly seemed like killers. Oh, and I met another friend of theirs, a Kevin Quinn. He seemed nice enough too. It was only once I started mingling with the supporters again that things got ugly. When I dropped my recorder, I got knocked to the ground. None of those people helped me up; they just glared at me like I was nothing but trash."

When she looked up again, she didn't miss the glance that passed between the three guys. "What?"

"Maybe Tim got one of his minions to do his dirty work," Vann said.

"I don't know," Geneva frowned. "Still seems like kind of a stretch. What if whoever he sent decided to go to the police instead? That's an awfully big risk for a guy like him to take. Maybe it was just construction failure."

"It was *not* construction failure," Mark said, coming to his buddy's defense. "I'm telling you, no one builds better than Jace. Nobody. If he said that structure was safe, then it was. It had to have been someone coming in afterward to do the damage."

"Think about it," Jace said. "When Mark's brakes went out, where were you guys? On Rigsdale property. Now, granted, it was an unexpected visit, but if Rigsdale put in a word with his minions that night—say spread the idea around to attack anyone who looked different than them—it's not such a huge leap to think one of those zealots might've cut your brake lines in the name of their cause, right?"

"I admit that's where my suspicions went after it happened," Mark said, shifting slightly in his hospital bed. The monitors continued to beep rhythmically around him, their drone oddly soothing. "Still it seems like a stretch to place Tim Rigsdale at the obstacle course. Not like the guy stops by every day for coffee and doughnuts."

"Not so." Vann rubbed his chin thoughtfully. "What about during the Strawberry Festival? Anyone could have come for the free tour of our compound, and just hidden somewhere until things died down."

"Shit, dude. You're right," Jace said.

Vann shook his head. "Hate to say it, but we couldn't ban them from the property. It was a public event. Besides, denying them access to the property without proof of ill intent hits me as way too close to the profiling they do to every non-white in the area. Trust me; I'll keep an eagle eye on them from now on though."

"Be careful." Mark scowled at the blank, white wall across the room. "If Tim Rigsdale *is* involved in this somehow, the last thing we want is for him to know we're on to his plan. We need to play things cool."

"Fine." Jace scrubbed a hand through his hair. "I'll talk to Ben later though."

"Who's Ben?" Geneva asked.

"My buddy on the local police force. He told me at the compound that the cops are going over to the mansion later this afternoon to ask the Rigsdales some questions. Afterward, I'll find out what they know." He glanced at Vann. "Sound good?"

Vann nodded. "Yeah, man. Sounds good."

"What about me? What can I do?" Geneva asked, not wanting to be left out.

Before the guys could answer, a knock sounded on the door.

"Mr. Rogers?" A petite Asian woman in a white lab coat entered the room. "I'm Dr. Forbes."

Mark gave a brief wave to the doctor then threw his legs over the side of the bed and started to stand, only to flop back down onto the edge of the bed, his hands shaking and his body swaying unsteadily.

"You need to stay in the hospital and rest, Mr. Rogers," Dr. Forbes advised. "At least overnight."

"I've got things to do."

"Mark, I think you should listen to the doctor." Geneva placed a hand on his arm. "Head injuries are nothing to mess around with. When Jaime came home from Kabul with—"

"You should listen to your girlfriend, Mr. Rogers." "Oh, I'm not his girlfriend," Geneva said.

"She's not my girlfriend," Mark said.

Jace and Vann shook their heads.

"Well, in that case, maybe everyone could leave the room while we talk?"

"Doc, anything you have to say, you can say in front of them," Mark responded.

"As you wish. In addition to your concussion, Mr. Rogers, you also have two fractured ribs and your left hand is broken in two places." Dr. Forbes studied his chart. "You need time to rest and recuperate. I'm sure whatever errands you need to run can wait until tomorrow, at least. I won't be discharging you until then at any rate. You'll require monitoring in case you develop a hematoma in your brain due to the concussion. If your brain bleeds and swells, it could kill you. Kind of puts things in perspective, eh?"

CHAPTER FIFTEEN

Geneva squeezed Mark's shoulder. Even though she'd only known him five days and they'd both adamantly denied the whole dating thing, her feelings for him were surprisingly strong. If he died, she wasn't sure how she'd handle that. She felt like she was only now emerging from the fog of grief Jaime's death had caused. To lose another person close to her might just kill her.

Mark squeezed her hand reassuringly then nodded. "Okay, doc. Whatever you say."

"I had an orthopedic surgeon look at the x-rays we took of your hand and you're a very lucky man. The fractures weren't offset and all your nerves are intact. Still, you need to be careful with it until it heals completely. One wrong move and you could lose some functionality in your fingers." Dr. Forbes set the chart aside, checked Mark's vitals once more, and then entered her results into the computer in the corner of the room. "I'll be back in to check on you again in the morning, Mr. Rogers. If you need anything at all tonight, please let one of the nurses know."

"Sure thing, doc." Mark flashed her a smile. "Thanks so much."

Geneva's suspicions rose. He seemed awfully agreeable all of a sudden.

Once the doctor left, Vann and Jace headed for the door as well. Jace's phone buzzed and he pulled it out. "Just got a text from Ben. Looks like they're heading to the mansion in an hour."

"Cool." Vann held the door for Jace then glanced back at Mark. "We'll call you when we're done. Rest up, buddy."

Mark nodded as they walked out then turned to Geneva. His normally tanned complexion held a tinge of gray. "Bet I look like twice-baked shit, huh?"

"Don't know about the twice-baked part." Geneva ran a gentle hand over his bruised cheek. "But you're pretty beat up. I'm glad you're okay though."

"Yeah?" He kissed her palm before letting her go. "I bet being here brings up painful memories for you, doesn't it? With your brother?"

She took a seat on the bed beside him. "This is the first time I've been back inside a hospital since—Jaime was in and out of psych wards for years. Each time he checked in, the stays got longer and more involved. More tests, more drugs, more therapy. It was all a bit overwhelming after a while."

"Didn't you have anyone else you could lean on for support?"

"Not really, no. My parents still live in Virginia and don't have the means to travel out here much. Besides, Jaime and I were always so close. I guess that's why I feel so strongly about helping him now. I can't fail him again, Mark. I just can't."

"Why do you think you failed him at all, *manamea*?" This time, he cupped her cheek with his uninjured hand, his thumb stroking gently over her skin. It took every ounce of willpower Geneva had not to scoot closer and sink into him, to let Mark take her burden, her guilt, at least for a little while. But she couldn't. Not until she'd finished this job. She owed that to Jaime. She owed that to herself. No matter how tempted her aching heart might be to surrender to her growing feelings for this man. She had to help people see that veterans weren't getting the help they needed when they came back from combat. She had to convince people the military—the government—needed to do more.

Mark sighed and narrowed his gaze on her. "Sounds to me like you did everything humanly possible to save your brother's life, Geneva."

"Everything except get him help sooner." She gave a sad little snort. "I can't help feeling that if I'd just paid more attention, kept a better watch on him, recognized the symptoms of his depression sooner, he might still be alive."

"You have no way of knowing that. None." Mark straightened in bed, cringing slightly when he jostled his sore ribs. "Jaime was a grown man, capable of making his own decisions. Plus, with his military background, his stoicism was drilled into him from day one. Believe me, I know. So, don't live your life based on what-ifs. It's a horrible waste. In Samoa, people believe in the circle of life, that everything happens for a reason and everything ties together to teach us the lessons we need to learn in the end."

Geneva managed not to roll her eyes, barely. Still, her pessimistic side couldn't let that one slide without comment. "What greeting card did you get that from?"

"Huh?" Mark scrunched his nose.

"Pretty words and inspirational quotes are fine and dandy, but they don't help much where real-life is concerned."

His expression shifted from concerned to stoic and his hand slid away from her face. "This is who I am, Geneva. I'm Samoan. Family is all-important to us, so believe me when I say that I understand your pain about losing your brother. But for you to close yourself off to the future and harden your heart because of what happened is ridiculous. I'm sure your brother would never have wanted that for you, *manamea.*"

His words hit far closer to the bone than she was willing to admit. Her wounds were still too fresh and her heart far too exposed. Geneva stood and moved to the far wall near the windows, her need to protect herself outweighing the truth of his words. "I'm not closed off or hardened to anything, Mark. I'm a realist. Pardon me for not getting all Hallmark Channel with you, okay?"

"You're scared." He tossed back the covers and moved to the edge of the bed again, sitting there a moment this time, eyes closed. "I get it. But I can't let Tim Rigsdale get away with this. I need to help the guys figure out what happened. I'm still their leader."

"You're not in the SEALs anymore, Mark." Geneva snorted. "Men are so stubborn. You can't even stand. The doctor just told you there might be life-threatening bleeding into your brain if you get out of bed. And yet you'll risk your own life when the guys already have a plan to handle things."

"Once a SEAL, always a SEAL. I can't sit by and do nothing. It wouldn't be right." Mark rose slowly onto his unsteady legs, clutching the bedrail for support as he swayed slightly on his feet. "I'd risk my life for Jace and Vann and they'd do the same for me. Always. That's the SEAL way."

Her combined frustration over his lack of compromise, the fact some unknown villain out there wanted to hurt him, and her failure to save her brother from cold, heartless military bureaucracy boiled over into rage. "You know what? Fuck the SEAL way."

"Don't you dare say that," Mark growled.

"Why? You think the SEAL way will save you if you end up brain damaged and alone in some psych ward at some washed up VA hospital because you refused to follow this doctor's orders, huh? Because, believe me, I've seen with my own eyes they won't." Incensed, Geneva strode over to the chair near the door where she'd dropped her purse on the way in. "Someone just tried to kill you Mark. And for all I know, maybe you weren't the first one either." Her reporter's brain bounced around the evidence with rapid-fire speed. "Hell, maybe those other SEAL deaths weren't suicides at all."

He frowned. "Keep your voice down."

Geneva blinked at him, stunned. "Oh my God. You don't think they were, do you?"

"I'm not sure, okay?" Mark said, his tone guarded. "I've been doing some investigation into the deaths of my two former employees, under the radar."

Fuck. The air in the room seemed to evaporate and the knot of anxiety coiled in her stomach pulled tighter. If what he said was true, if he'd uncovered proof the two deaths were murders and not suicides, then this was the chance she'd been waiting for, the opportunity to dig deeper, get the story of a lifetime if she could prove a power couple like the Rigsdales were somehow behind all of this. She should be running out the door, tackling this investigation head on. And yet, all she wanted to do at that moment was apologize to the man she'd just insulted to his very core. She exhaled, hesitating. "I need to go."

"That's it? I can't believe you're running away from this."

"I am not running away." Each word gritted out of her sandpaper dry throat, brittle as glass. "I just need some air."

"Air. Right." Teeth clenched, Mark ripped out his IV and the monitors beside him went wild. Tore off the wires connecting him to various machines. Even battered and bruised, he was still the most gorgeous man she'd ever seen—all sleek muscle and corded sinew wrapped in an exquisite mocha-skinned package. He limped over to the armoire to pull out his clothes and glanced over, catching her staring. Geneva looked away quick.

She heard, rather than saw, him tug on his jeans then curse. Geneva looked over her shoulder in time to see him tip sideways. Hunched, Mark leaned one hand against the armoire door while holding his forehead with the other.

"Maybe you should get back in bed," Geneva said. Without thinking, she rushed to his side to help.

"Maybe you should mind your own business." He shook off her touch. "Why won't you ever take off those damned boots?"

Flinching, Geneva looked down at her feet then back at him. She'd never let anyone see her deformity. Not since she was ten and her best friend betrayed her secret—she had six toes on her right foot. The other kids had called her a freak, bullied her to the point that her parents had to pull her out of school.

Surgery would've been the easiest solution, at least as far as Geneva was concerned, but her parents encouraged her to keep it. They'd always taught her to accept that not everyone was perfect nor were they all the same. That sometimes life's imperfections are more obvious than others are and it was up to us to learn to accept them rather than sit in judgment.

While Geneva had worked hard to be accepting that, she was different, children could be cruel and every time she thought about revealing her secret, she was suddenly that ten-year-old little girl again and she could hear the taunts in her head. Now, the extra toe had become a crutch, one more reason she used to keep from getting too close to anyone. The fact Mark had picked up on her weakness so quickly, especially after years of concealment, only made Geneva's anxiety worse. Scrambling to throw him off track, she backed toward the door again. "I like these boots."

"I like chocolate too. Doesn't mean I eat it every second of every damned day." Mark took a deep breath then zipped up his fly before tugging his company polo shirt over his head. He cringed and held his side, not looking at her. "I'm done, Geneva. Just go."

Mark slumped carefully down into the chair on the other side of his bed to put on his socks and shoes.

"You're leaving, aren't you? Against the doctor's orders." Geneva gripped the doorframe, the cold metal cutting into her skin. "That's the stupidest thing I've ever heard. What about your friends, huh? They're worried about you."

"Yeah? And what about you, Geneva? Are you worried about me too?" He sat forward, his legs spread, elbows resting on his knees while his hands hung limp between them. His fingers were visibly shaking from his minor efforts. She wanted to respond, wanted to tell him that yes, she was worried about him. That yes, she wanted nothing more than to cuddle up in his arms and never leave his side, but the words stuck in her throat. She had to remember her priorities, her reason for being here. Jaime. Jaime needed her to fight this last battle for him, needed her to win this war even though he'd lost his personal battle with his demons.

At her silence, Mark exhaled, sad and slow. "Go, Geneva. We're done."

Heartbroken, she stared at him for a small eternity. Part of her wanted to rush back to his side, to sit with him and make sure he didn't do anything stupid, like check himself out of the hospital against his doctor's orders. Unfortunately, the other part of her— the one hardened by her past and determined to stay firmly planted in reality, for her brother's sake—wouldn't let her. Pulse pounding in her ears and bile rising in her throat from her churning stomach, Geneva gave Mark a last long look before turning away. "Fine. Goodbye. Be careful."

CHAPTER SIXTEEN

Mark sat alone for a moment, eyes closed and head throbbing, summoning every ounce of willpower he had to struggle to his feet once more. Discharging himself was a bad idea, he knew that, but what the hell else was he supposed to do? Sit around while someone tried to hurt or kill his friends and other fellow SEALs?

Not happening.

Those guys were part of his family, his *Aiga*, and he'd meant what he'd said to Geneva. For him, family was everything. Openness and honesty rated close seconds. Wisdom said he should forget about her, let her do her job and he'd do his and that would be the end of it. But still his heart ached at the way they'd just ended things.

Pardon me for not getting all Hallmark Channel with you…

Geneva's earlier snark made him chuckle despite himself.

Okay. It was a good comeback. He could admit it.

After a deep breath, Mark raised his head and waited for his balance to stabilize before pushing to his feet once more. The world went cockeyed a bit at first, but if he didn't make any sudden moves, he'd be fine. Plus, he'd stop at the gift store on the way out and buy some Dramamine to settle his stomach. Good as new.

Mark grabbed his wallet from the nightstand drawer where the nurse had stashed it when they'd moved him from the ER after his scan, then made his way out into the busy hall and over to the nurses' station.

"I'm checking myself out of here," he said to the woman behind the desk. Her nametag said Rose. "Thanks for all your hard work, Rose."

She eyed him warily. "What room are you in, Mr...?"

"Rogers. Mark Rogers." He flashed her what he hoped was his best flirty smile. "And that one over there."

"Room 201." She shifted through a stack of charts in a bin in front of her then pulled one out with his name emblazoned in one corner. "This says Dr. Forbes has ordered a twenty-four-hour admit for you."

"I'm feeling much better and I really have to get home." His smile faded slightly as his head ached. Ibuprofen. He mentally added that to his must-buy list from the pharmacy downstairs. "So, if you could just give me the paperwork to sign, I'd appreciate it."

"Early discharge isn't recommended, Mr. Rogers. You have a pretty nasty concussion. Checking out against doctor's orders could have severe consequences." Rose scowled at her computer screen as she typed. "Plus, you don't look so good either."

"I'm fine." He gripped the edge of her counter tight. "If you could hurry, please, I've got somewhere I need to be. You can't keep me here against my will. I know my rights."

Rose gave a long-suffering sigh then stood and walked to a nearby printer. She plucked a paper from it, then returned and placed the form and a pen in front of him. "Sign here and date it. This states you know the risks and are choosing to discharge yourself anyway."

"Thanks." Mark squinted down at the dotted line—it doubled, then tripled, before returning to one solid line. He blinked hard and scribbled what he hoped would pass for his signature before passing the form back to her. "Have an awesome day, Rose."

"Want me to call a cab?" she called from behind him.

"That would be perfect. Thanks."

Behind him, Rose mumbled something that sounded suspiciously like *Idiot*.

By the time Mark stopped at the pharmacy then made his way outside, he did feel marginally better. The fresh air made his head feel clearer and his balance had improved. The two pain pills and the stomach remedy he'd taken with a swallow of water from the drinking fountain inside hadn't hurt either. The sun still shone above though the breeze had turned colder this late in the afternoon.

He waited at the curb until his cab arrived, then climbed into the backseat and gave the driver directions to take him to the compound. With luck, Vann would have more information on the dome collapse and Jace would have talked to his friend with the police department. Together, the three of them could talk through this shit storm and come up with a plan of attack.

As he slipped on his sunglasses around his bandages, he winced. He hadn't meant to let Geneva know about his suspicions regarding the suicides. Not until he was sure what he was dealing with, though he supposed after what had happened today she'd connect the dots sooner or later anyway. Considering he didn't plan to see her again now, it wouldn't matter. Regret pinched his heart before he could stop it. He and Geneva had slept together twice, but hadn't known each other that long. It shouldn't hurt to let her go, shouldn't bother him to say goodbye to her, and yet....

Mark shook off his melancholy as best he could and concentrated on the road ahead.

Must be the medications making him sappy.

Someday he'd find the right woman, someone who didn't lie or try to get closer to him under false pretenses. A woman who loved him for who he was, a woman who looked on the bright side of life like him, a woman who always told him the truth and kept her heart open to him no matter what happened.

Traffic seemed heavier than usual, so the drive to the compound was slow going, but it was just as well. The last thing Mark needed right now was a case of whiplash from an overeager cab driver to put him right back in the hospital. As they travelled the few miles from Ortega General back to Brothers In Arms, his mind spun with what had occurred today. If Vann and Jace turned up more proof that Tim Rigsdale had been involved in the dome collapse, then that might be the missing piece he needed to go to the police with his theory about Rick and Jon's suicides not being suicides at all—and if the police opened an investigation, that might be enough to convince the life insurance company to reopen the cases for their families as well.

Feeling more hopeful, Mark settled back in his seat. With his left hand swaddled in bandages and splinted, he couldn't do much with it. Out the window, he spied the cliffs rising on either side of him as they headed out of Ortega proper.

Yep. Leaving the hospital had been the best decision.

Minutes later, the driver pulled into the compound parking lot and stopped near the office. Mark paid his fare then limped the short distance to his office. His head felt clearer now, if still sore. His left hand throbbed too, along with his ribs meaning the pain meds he got in the hospital were wearing off. All the better. He wanted to be alert and clear-headed when he talked to the guys about what they'd discovered.

Inside his office, Mark took a seat, and then found himself unable to concentrate. Not because of his injuries, but because of that spot on his desk—the one where he'd made love to Geneva. God, he honestly couldn't remember the sex ever being that good with anyone else.

Gah! He scrubbed his good hand over his face. Maybe he had acted like a dick about those stupid boots she always wore, but shit. His dad used to do the same thing. Always blowing up over the tiniest, stupidest things. He'd told her upfront that openness and truth were the most important things to him and yet she couldn't even trust him enough to tell him about something as simple as her clothing choices. And if Geneva had lied to him about that, what was to stop her from lying about big things too?

Fuck it. Just fuck it all to hell and back.

He'd been there done the whole lying thing with his father. He wasn't doing that again.

Ever.

No matter how gorgeous and funny and smart and talented and awesome Geneva was.

With a sigh, Mark slumped back in his chair. It was better this way, better they'd gone their separate ways, ended it when they had at the hospital earlier.

Mark tried to finish up some accounting paperwork left over from the night before and enter the registrations from the class they'd cancelled today because of the collapse, moving the enrolled students to the next available class the following week or issuing refunds when necessary, but it was hard. Typing with one hand was inconvenient as hell. His head throbbed and his thoughts were fuzzy and his vision kept blurring the longer he stared down at those damned numbers and…

"Jesus, man. What the hell are you doing here?" Jace said as he and Vann walked into the office. "You're supposed to be resting in your hospital room."

"Can't do that." Mark scowled down at the stack of papers in front of him. "What did you guys find out?"

"Not much," Vann said. He'd pulled his hair out of the ponytail he had in the hospital and resembled a Cherokee warrior on the hunt even more than usual. His current dour expression didn't help the situation. "Ben said the Rigsdales had their fancy attorney present and refused to answer any questions."

"What else is new?" Mark snorted.

"I did get a chance to have Ben poke around a bit though," Jace said. "He said he found some interesting tools in their garage."

"Like what?" Mark asked.

"Like handsaws and cutting shears that would be perfect for sawing through the boards on our Diesel Dome."

"That doesn't prove anything, really." Mark shook his head. "Everybody's got a saw in their toolbox."

"Does Tim Rigsdale look like the kind of guy who uses hand tools to you?" Vann asked, his tone flat.

"Good point. But they've probably got handymen on staff, right?" Mark narrowed his gaze. "What about the wife? Did Kim say anything?"

"Other than all her toxic bullshit about the minorities in town taking over everything?" Vann shrugged. "Nope. But Ben still thinks they're hiding something. Or someone. I took a drive up there, after we left the police station. Stayed hidden until the coast was clear, and then searched the dirt surrounding their garage in the back. There were three sets of footprints. That third set didn't match either of the Rigsdales. The size was bigger, indicating a taller man, and deeper, meaning he would've been heavier, muscled maybe."

"So you think they're covering for someone else?" Mark asked. "Or maybe they've hired someone to do their dirty work?"

"Hiring someone would make more sense," Jace said. "Honestly, Tim Rigsdale has the book smarts to figure out the plans for something like the Diesel Dome collapse, but he's pretty scrawny. Can't see him climbing around all over that thing to make the needed *adjustments*. Can you?"

"Shit. That doesn't help me at all." Mark pushed to his feet and headed across his office to his gun cabinet. With his left hand fucked up, he'd need to pack a lighter weapon that he could draw, aim, and fire with just his right, should the need arise. "I'm going up there myself."

"Wait a minute," Vann stood and walked over to Mark, taking him by the arm. "The only place you need to go is back to the hospital, buddy."

"Fuck the hospital. The longer it takes to get the evidence we need to go to the police about the murders, the more Rick and Jon's families suffer. They're living below the poverty level as it is. I have to do what I can to help them."

"Perfect." Vann threw his hands up, his expression exasperated. "And you think killing yourself will help the situation? Listen, you drive up there to the mansion guns blazing and cap them all in the ass one-handed, and that will only ensure the cops never reopen the case. No new investigation. No reopening of the case for the families. Is that what you want, huh?"

"Maybe. No. Just shut the hell up." Mark jammed a full magazine into the Glock he'd chosen then twisted to buckle on his waist holster. Fresh agony zinged up from his cracked ribs and he did his best to hide his discomfort, though couldn't quiet conceal his wince. "Don't worry about me."

"What about the rest of us, huh, man?" Jace said, joining them. "We're involved in this too. All three of us are equal partners in the business, Mark. If you get yourself killed and Brothers In Arms fails, so do we. You don't think Vann and I want to catch whoever did this just as bad as you do?"

"You're not the one they tried to kill today," Mark said, his anger rising. Truth was, he felt like shit, and he wasn't in the mood for a lecture about his health and choices right now. "I'm going up there and that's it. We need to hit this head on and nip whatever plans they have in the bud."

"How about a little finesse instead? What about Geneva? She could get us in there with her press credentials, right?" Vann asked, arms crossed, blocking Mark's exit to the door. From the dots of crimson on his high cheekbones and hard edge in his black eyes, he was every bit as pissed as Mark. "Charging onto their property and pulling a Rambo isn't going to help the situation."

"No. Geneva's out of the picture, okay?" Mark attempted to push past his buddies. When that failed, he headed back to his desk instead and pretended to shuffle through some papers. "We'll have to figure out a way to get onto the Rigsdales' property ourselves. If you guys won't help me, then I'll go by myself."

Mark headed for the door again and managed to dodge Vann this time.

His triumph was short-lived, however, when Jace followed him out into the parking lot. "C'mon, man. The Rigsdales are rich. They've got law enforcement and politicians in their pockets. There's no way this works out well for you. For any of us. Let's go back inside and talk this out. The way we used to back in Kabul. There's no problem we can't solve if we put our heads together."

Mark stopped near the Humvee and kicked the tire hard in frustration. *Fuck.* Much as he hated to admit it, Jace was right. He was going off half-cocked. The ache in his head worsened and his stomach roiled and all he wanted to do at that moment was close his eyes and sleep for days.

After a deep breath to steady himself, he turned slowly to face the guys. "Fine. I'll stay here for now. But we need to hash out a plan to handle this cluster fuck. And then I need a nap."

CHAPTER SEVENTEEN

Mark woke up on the couch in his office a few hours later. Jace was snoozing in a chair across from him and Vann had left a note taped to Mark's chest stating he was headed home to his apartment in town. Mark yawned then winced at his sore ribs. The guys had insisted on staying with him, because of the concussion, so they'd decided to take round-the-clock shifts through the night to make sure he didn't kick the bucket.

Stretching cautiously, he gingerly rolled over onto his back and squinted at the clock on the wall above his desk. It was nearly six p.m. His stomach rumbled. They'd worked through the afternoon coming up with a strategy to deal with Tim Rigsdale and whoever else the guy might have working for him. At least they were going to be proactive about it from this point forward. More investigation into Rick and Jon's deaths, more face time with the Rigsdales to make sure they knew Brothers In Arms, and Mark in particular, wouldn't put up with their crap anymore. Enough was enough. Time to make the truth known.

He rubbed a hand over his face and stared at the ceiling. Vann had brought up another good point during their discussion about the suicides that they now suspected weren't suicides at all. One of the pre-requisites of entering SEAL training was a psych evaluation. They only took the most dedicated, most well-adapted guys into the program. Anyone who didn't have the stamina or the mental toughness to handle what the job required was weeded out quickly. And SEALs took care of their own. Plus, the teams usually stayed close, even after they came home. For random ex-SEALs to start offing themselves because of a lack of support didn't make sense.

The phone in his pocket buzzed and Mark wriggled slightly to pull it out of his jeans pocket then squinted at the screen. A message from his sister flashed brightly:

Need to see you ASAP.

Scoops

L

Shit. Vann had said he'd called them. Most likely Leila and Mom had gone to the hospital to see him, only to find him already gone. One thing was certain. His sister wasn't happy.

Slowly, Mark sat up, his hand against his injured ribs to keep from jostling them. The sooner he got back into his regular routine, the better. Plus, staying busy would help him forget about losing Geneva. That was the theory anyway.

At least the dizziness seemed to have subsided and his head hurt less, which was good. And, given everything else going on, it wasn't a bad idea to check in on his family to make sure she and Mom were okay, let them see that he was okay too. Over the past week or so, he hadn't exactly been spending as much time with them as he usually did.

Maybe Leila had run another massive root beer float sale and she'd run short on supplies again. Mark snorted. Seemed his sister was always promoting the crap out of something at her store these days.

He pushed to his feet, careful to stay as quiet as possible to avoid waking Jace. There were dark circles under his buddy's eyes and the guy needed the rest almost as much as Mark did. On sock-covered feet, he tiptoed toward the bathroom door in the corner of his office. Once he'd taken care of business, he checked his reflection in the mirror, and then wished he hadn't. God, that fall had done a number on him. There was a nasty gash on his cheek and a fresh bruise on his forehead, not to mention the ever-attractive, mummy-like bandage on his skull.

Mark shook his head and washed his hands, then headed back out into the office. Jace was still sprawled out in his seat, snoring loudly. Poor guy. No need to wake him. He scribbled a quick note then placed the sticky note on Jace's chest, same as Vann had done for him. With luck, Mark could make the quick run to Leila's, help her with whatever she needed, then come back here before Jace even knew he'd been gone.

Keys in hand, he exited the office and strode across the parking lot to the Humvee. The sun was setting over the Pacific in the distance and the sky was tinged with glorious shades of red, orange and indigo. It was so beautiful it made his heart ache. He started to wish Geneva were here to see it with him before he stopped himself. They were done. Time to move on.

Heart heavy despite his resolve to forget her, Mark climbed in behind the wheel of the Humvee and cranked the engine. Tourist traffic was surprisingly light on Highway 1 and with the warm breeze blowing, he left the windows down as he cruised along the ocean-side highway heading back into Ortega. In the gathering twilight, it was almost possible to forget about all the nasty shit going down in the world, all the people like the Rigsdales, and that asshole Sutton running for Congress. Hell, now that he felt moderately better, he could almost even forget that someone had tried to kill him earlier—and damned near succeeded too. Mark glanced into the rearview mirror then slowed down as he approached a sharper curve in the road ahead.

Headlights loomed behind him, closer than necessary.

Dumbass tailgaters. Probably some lost tourist fighting with his wife. Mark snorted and kept to the right-hand side, hoping the moron would go ahead and pass him.

No such luck. As he approached another curve and Mark tapped his brakes again, the vehicle behind him revved its engine and drew even closer to the Humvee's bumper.

Cursing, Mark leaned out the drivers' side window. He couldn't flip them off like he wanted with his hand all taped up, but he gave them a curt wave just the same.

Assholes. Always in a hurry.

He sat back and pressed the gas pedal a little harder, hoping maybe he could lose the guy. Except the faster he went, the closer the guy seemed to get. With sheer cliffs on one side of him, dropping off into the Pacific, and nothing but miles of foothills on the other, there wasn't any place for him to go but straight ahead. In the distance, he could see the twinkling lights of downtown Ortega beckoning. Then the glare of the other vehicles headlights filled the interior of his car once more.

This time the guy was close enough that the roar of his engine was nearly deafening.

Mark gripped the steering wheel tight with his right hand and forced his tense muscles to relax. Whatever happened, he'd handle it. He'd been trained in evasive maneuvers. Even if the guy tried to—

WHAM!

No more "if" about it. Whoever was driving that car was after Mark.

The other car behind him rammed hard into the back of the Humvee, sending Mark skidding into the opposite lane of traffic. Thankfully, there wasn't anything coming or he would've been in serious jeopardy for the second time that day. He managed to gain control of the massive Humvee and eased back into his lane.

The problem with huge SUVs like the one he was driving wasn't that they couldn't take a hit. Hell, the damned things were military grade. Humvee's were built like damned tanks. The problem was when the weight distribution inside shifted abruptly, increasing the risk of rollover. When they converted the Humvee to civilian use, they'd put bigger tires on them, which also displaced their center of gravity. So, taking a Humvee head-on was unnecessary when all that was really needed was catch a back corner just right and tip the whole thing over.

Fuck.

Barreling down the two-lane highway, Mark did his best to outrun whoever was behind him, but speed wasn't exactly the Humvee's forte either.

BANG!

He jolted forward again as the other vehicle rammed him a second time and pain burst up his left side from his cracked ribs. Memories of Geneva and her disapproval over him discharging himself swamped Mark's adrenaline-soaked mind. Given how his evening was going, maybe staying in the hospital overnight wouldn't have been such a bad idea after all. He would've chuckled at the irony, if he wasn't frantically trying to save his own life. Again.

The last curve before hitting Ortega town proper loomed ahead and it was of the hairpin variety. Logically, Mark knew his best chance of escaping his pursuers was to lose them in that curve. All he had to do was slow down a little before the entry…

Those thoughts didn't help to slow his hammering pulse or stop his throat from constricting to the point it made it hard to swallow. Hands shaking with stress, he said a silent prayer.

Alii e, fesoasoani mai ia te au… Lord, help me.

He eased off the gas a bit and held his breath.

Waiting, waiting, waiting…

Then Mark punched the accelerator as he headed into the curve. He'd lived in Ortega all his life and driven that stretch of highway more times than he could count. He should've been able to do this with his eyes closed. Unfortunately, he'd never done the curve with a head injury or with another car barreling up his ass at close to ninety miles per hour.

Using all his muscles, he held the wheel as steady as he could, but there was no stopping the Humvee as it veered toward the foothills. *Better than the ocean plunge on the right*, he thought absently as time blew by in a blur.

His wheels skidded on the gravel of the berm then he zoomed headlong into the brush, down into a gulley and back up the other side before tipping over completely and landing on the drivers' side of the vehicle in a *whoosh* of dirt. Mark's already battered head slammed hard against the ground through the open window and knocked him loopy for a second. All he heard through his hazy, muddled thoughts was the whine of the still running engine, the scratch of the dry grass against his sore cheek, the voices from somewhere in the distance.

Unfamiliar, male voices.

He struggled to hear what they were saying, but his pulse was pounding and his vision was tunneling. His mouth felt dry as a bone and his injured left hand throbbed anew. Seems he'd somehow landed on top of it. Mark groaned, the sound echoing inside the Humvee as he struggled to undo his seatbelt and found he couldn't—the fingers of his left hand refused to work. Ah, shit. Doctor Forbes words from earlier reverberated alongside the heartbeat in his head.

One wrong move and you could lose part of the functionality...

He made his living with his hands. If he lost the use of one of them, what would he do?

Headlights blazed through the shattered windshield as his assailant's car pulled to a stop near the wreckage.

Panic joined the adrenaline already flooding Mark's system and the darkness around him crowded closer. A loud metallic creak sliced through the night as the passenger side door of the Humvee was wrenched open and the bright beam of a flashlight blinded him.

Eyes squinted, Mark tried to discern who his attackers were, but all he could make out were vague silhouettes.

"Get him out of there," a man said. "And make sure he doesn't remember shit about you."

"Yes, sir," another voice answered.

Mark's last vision was a fist flying directly at his face, smashing hard into his jaw, then nothing.

CHAPTER EIGHTEEN

Mark came to slowly, his vision blurry and his body aching. He was bouncing.

Why the fuck was he bouncing?

It took him a minute to realize he wasn't bouncing. He was being carried, by four huge guys in black suits, down an ornate marble hallway. His heavy eyes closed again.

Where the hell am I and how did I end up here?

His last memories were waking up in his office, getting the text from Leila, and then sneaking out while Jace slept to go to Scoops. He tried to shake his head, but found that only made the dizziness and aching worse and upset his stomach, so he remained still. Each guy had him by an extremity as they toted him to God knew where. Mark peeked one eye open again and spotted expensive artwork on the walls and crystal chandeliers twinkling from the ceiling above. The air smelled of candle wax, pine-scented cleaner, and lavender potpourri.

His handlers turned a corner then hauled him into what appeared to be a huge library. Floor to ceiling bookshelves lined the walls and were stuffed to the brim with reading material. They tossed him down onto a musty old Persian rug amidst the shouts of what sounded like one hell of a fight between the room's other occupants, whom he couldn't quite see from his position. Curses that would make a sailor blush flew and he realized one of the voices was female. At least he'd had sense enough to turn his head before his body hit the floor, saving him from face-planting, but the awkward way he'd come to rest didn't do anything to help him figure out who was doing the yelling. Luckily, he didn't have to wait long to find out.

Moments later a pair of designer stilettos stalked into his view, along with the same shrill voice he'd heard countless times during various American Way protests around Ortega.

Kim Rigsdale.

Pulse kicking higher, Mark did his best to stay still and play dead while he listened in on their fight, but damn. They'd been right. The Rigsdales were responsible. The reasons why still weren't concrete, but he sure as hell intended to find out.

"What the hell are you doing?" Kim yelled from above him. "You guys can't just drop him on my priceless antique rug! Those bloodstains will never come out. Not to mention the trace evidence this leaves in my house." She nudged Mark's arm with the pointy tip of her shoe. "Oh, wonderful. And now he's bled on my new sofa too. Goddammit, Tim! Clean up your fucking mess!"

"My mess? Since when did this shit become my mess, huh? Fuck you, Kim. Last time I checked, we were both in this together." Tim's steps pounded over as he joined his wife near

172

Mark's head. "You knew exactly what we were getting into when we signed on to do this. Don't even think about trying to lay all the blame for this fucking mess on me now." Tim mumbled something Mark didn't quite catch then turned slightly to face the other side of the room. "Can't we just shoot him in the head and dump his body in the flatlands somewhere. Just make it look like a suicide like the other ones?"

Mark's pulse stumbled.

The other ones? The other deaths? Rick and Jon?

"Calm down," a new male voice said, one Mark hadn't heard before. "If we do that, we blow all the groundwork we've accomplished so far. We need to be rational about this. We kill him now and dump him; the cops are going to get suspicious. They were just here questioning you, remember?"

"He's right, dammit," Kim said, her tone annoyed. "But I really don't have time to play nursemaid. I've got the Ladies for Democracy rally to plan for next week and I'm holding another fundraising luncheon for Sutton's female supporters here on Friday. I can't have a bloody, beat-up black guy stuffed inside one of my closets."

Mark wanted to yell that he wasn't African-American, but bit his tongue. Instead, he clenched his jaw and focused on filing away every word they'd said. He'd need those details to relay to the police and the guys later.

If there is a later…

"What about the new wine cellar? Is it finished yet?" the new guy asked.

"No," Tim exhaled loudly. "The construction company's way over deadline on it and now they informed me they're taking the rest of the week off for mandatory OSHA training. I think it's all a bunch of horseshit."

"More like perfect." The new guy walked over to join the Rigsdales, his black combat boots entering Mark's line of vision. Standard issue military, available at any supply store or online. Not hugely helpful in identifying the guy, but at least he knew whoever the new guy was; he was most likely a vet or liked to dress like one. "We can lock him up in the wine cellar, away from everyone and everything, until he heals up a bit. No one will hear him if he screams and no one will look for him there. Once the police have put this whole dome collapse accident to rest, then he'll turn up dead in the ocean with a note. Just one more unfortunate suicide."

Mark's blood ran cold. Momentary triumph over having his suspicions confirmed mingled with horror at what had befallen his comrades.

The nearby sofa creaked as Tim sank down onto it. "I don't know…"

"Don't go all soft on me now, goddammit," the new guy growled, all civility gone from his tone. "We had a deal. I've fulfilled my end. Now it's up to you guys to do your part. Keep your end of the deal or I swear to fucking God you'll end up fish food just like those other useless fuckers."

"Tim?" Kim said, her confident tone now quivering with fear.

"Fine." Tim sighed loud. "Grab him and follow me. But I want it on record I'm not comfortable with this."

"Whatever," the new guy said, stepping aside as the four body guards moved in beside Mark to pick him up again.

Mark's thoughts raced as the thugs carted him out of the room. Facing the floor now, he couldn't see much of the route they were taking this time, just a bunch of plastic tarps and building supplies. The air turned cooler as they passed through another doorway and headed down a flight of stairs to an underground wine cellar.

"Put him over there," Tim said.

The guards tossed Mark across the room where he landed atop a pile of white canvas tarps. His entire left side protested and he had to bite back a groan of pain. One of the bodyguards threw something down beside him before they left. The sound of the lock grinding shut echoed through the dank space and one bare bulb glowed and buzzed from the ceiling. From somewhere in the shadows came the sound of a slow, monotonous drip.

He sat up slowly, keeping his head down for a moment while he regained his equilibrium. He peered around the space. Some wine cellar. Nothing but building supplies, no vino. He patted his pockets, hoping to find his phone, but nothing. Either the guards had found it or it was still back in the Humvee.

Talk about shitty luck.

After rubbing his eyes, Mark glanced beside him at what the guards had left. A broken cell phone, the screen cracked and smashed. A very familiar looking cell phone. He picked it up and flipped it over, recognizing the engraving on the back immediately and his nerves jangled anew. *Well, shit.*

It was Leila's.

His inner tension ratcheted higher still, if that were possible. His sister. His only sister. *Jesus Christ Almighty.* If those bastards so much as laid a finger on his LeLi, he'd fucking kill them with his bare hands. No one messed with his family. No one.

Mark pushed to his feet and promptly smacked his already sore head on the low, stone ceiling.

Dammit.

Cursing a blue streak and hunched over, he tromped around the space.

There had to be a way out of here.

He made his way back up the stone stairs to the door. Mark tried the handle just in case, but it was locked. Then he used his shoulder to ram it, hoping to bust it down. Fresh agony rippled up his side from his cracked ribs and his vision blurred with the effort to remain on his feet. The solid pine didn't budge an inch. Leave it to the fucking Rigsdales to buy the best.

Frustrated and furious, he headed back downstairs and searched through the piles of construction supplies, thinking maybe the builders had left a spare key or some power tools he might be able to use to escape. Nada. All he found was a black leather pouch with a few small screwdrivers and files. Too small to help with the door. Defeat rushing him from all sides, Mark sank back down to sit on the pile of tarps and stared at Leila's jacked-up cell phone.

Man, things were fucked up this time. That guy with the Rigsdales had been right. Down here, no one would find him and no one would hear his cries for help. He was on his own.

Shit. Just shit.

He scrubbed his right hand over the bandages on his head. God, he prayed Leila was okay, that they'd just stolen her phone and not hurt her. Eyes closed, he drew his knees into his chest and rested his forehead on them. She could be in dire trouble and there wasn't anything he could do to help her.

I'm so sorry, LeLi.

Images of her the day of his birthday party filled Mark's overtaxed mind. The way she'd tried to make the day special for him, the way she'd told him off afterward, and called him out on his bad behavior. *Fuck.* Mark sighed. She'd been right about him too. He did hold other people to his impossibly high standards, but not himself. Hell, just look what happened with Geneva.

Geneva.

His chest squeezed with remorse and regret.

This was his fault. All his fault. He blinked at the damaged cell phone again. It had cost him a shot at happily ever after. Now, it might very well cost him and his sister their lives too.

Think, Aleki. Think. Don't you dare give up on me now.

LeLi's voice echoed through his head, as clear as if she were standing before him. The thought of never seeing her smiling face again, never seeing his beloved mother, never seeing Geneva and apologizing to her, never seeing the guys again, was unbearable. Those people were everything to him—worth any pain, worth any sacrifice, worth any risk.

Mark opened his eyes and picked up the damaged cell phone, cradling it in his bandaged left hand. Jace had shown him one time how to rig one of these things in case of an emergency. As long as the inner components hadn't been demolished, you could rewire them to send a final SOS call.

With his good right hand, he grabbed the small packet of tools he'd found earlier and pulled out a tiny screwdriver. He might be trapped in this underground shithole and temporarily down for the count, but fuck all if he would give up without a fight.

CHAPTER NINETEEN

Geneva checked out of the Fireside Inn and finished jamming her suitcase into the back of her SUV. So far, this story idea had been a bust and it wasn't looking like things would improve any time soon, given the way she'd left things with Mark at the hospital.

Much as she hated to throw in the towel, it was time to head home and regroup.

She tamped down the wave of sadness that rose at the idea of leaving Mark and her hopes to help Jaime behind, even temporarily. She blinked up at the waxing moon above and blinked away the unexpected sting of tears. Crying now wouldn't help anything.

Lots of people hated driving at night, but Geneva loved it. Less traffic, cooler temps, better tunes and podcasts on the satellite radio. What wasn't to love? She climbed into the drivers' seat and started her engine then sat back in her seat and sighed.

Dammit. Ever since she'd left the hospital she'd had the gnawing feeling something wasn't right. It went beyond the fact she wasn't happy about how she'd left things with Mark—that was a whole other cesspool of emotions right there. Nope. It had more to do with his revelation about the suicides not being suicides at all.

With a sigh, Geneva flipped on her headlights then pulled out of the parking lot. As she drove through the evening lights of downtown Ortega, she couldn't help slowing as she approached Scoops. The lights were still on inside, which meant Leila was still there. Geneva found herself signaling and turning into the small lot before she'd even realized what she was doing.

Okay, yes. Maybe things hadn't ended well between her and Mark. Didn't mean she couldn't say goodbye to his sister and say thanks for the hospitality she'd shown her on her first day in town. Besides, Geneva genuinely liked Leila. Maybe they could even be friends on her next jaunt through Ortega.

She got out of the SUV and walked up to the door. It was locked, of course, given closing time was nine p.m., nearly an hour prior. She tapped on the door anyway, spotting Leila behind the ice cream counter. Mark's sister waved and jogged over to the entrance to let her in.

"Hey, how are you?" Leila asked as Geneva walked into the now deserted restaurant.

"Good. Sorry to bother you after work."

"No problem. I'm just cleaning up and prepping for tomorrow. Got behind after Mark's accident earlier. I went to see him at the hospital, but he'd already checked himself out. I called his cell and left messages for him right after I got back here, but then I got busy and haven't had time to check in on him again." Leila gestured for Geneva to follow her back over to the ice cream counter. "Typical man. Can't sit still for more than two seconds. You've seen him though, right? Is he okay?"

"Yeah." Geneva forced a smile, her chest aching with regret. She hoped Mark was okay, hoped he was following the doctor's orders to rest, though she knew that was probably asking the impossible. "I saw him at the hospital. He was banged up pretty bad, but he'll live."

"I'd offer you something to drink, but I've already shut everything down," Leila said, bustling around behind the counter. "We could stop by my mom's restaurant after this though, if you don't have plans. She'd love to meet you."

"I'm actually leaving tonight."

"Where are you going?" Leila stopped and faced Geneva, an ice cream scoop in one hand.

"Back to San Francisco."

"So soon?" Leila tossed the scoop into a gray plastic vat of soapy water and wiped her hands on a towel at her waist. "Why?"

"My sources aren't really panning out and I need some time to readjust and regroup."

"It's my brother, isn't it?" Leila put her hands on her hips and frowned. "Mark's so damned stubborn. I told him not to blow things with you and what does he do? Blows things sky high like a frigging volcano. Talk about needing to take his own advice."

Geneva didn't respond. Mark wasn't the only one who needed to walk his talk. She should've just told him about her stupid toes. She was an adult woman—smart, accomplished, attractive. If some guy couldn't deal with her imperfections, then screw him.

Except those old childhood wounds were never far from the surface and those horrid taunts of the bullies still echoed in her head late at night when she was all alone. Alone without Mark. Heartsick, she swallowed hard against the lump of sadness in her throat. "Anyway, I just wanted to stop by on my way out of Ortega and say thanks for being so kind to me that first day. You were really great."

"Aw, you're welcome. I loved meeting you." Leila took off her apron and headed for the cash register area. "Let's at least exchange cell phone numbers and maybe we can get together one day when I'm off. Winter's my slow time so…" She reached under the counter and grabbed her bag. "Plus, with this hectic place, I don't get a chance to make many new friends. When I'm not working, I'm home with the hubs and kids." She unzipped her purse and rooted around then scowled. "Aw, shit."

"What's wrong?" Geneva walked over to where she stood near the entrance.

"My phone's missing." Leila dumped the contents of her bag out onto the counter and sorted through it all, but no phone. "I don't usually leave my stuff lying around out here but I was in a hurry after my wasted trip to the hospital and didn't have time to stow it in my office like I usually do. Crap. Mark had that specially engraved for me too."

"Here, give me your number," Geneva said, pulling out her own phone. "I can call you. Maybe it just fell out around here somewhere."

"Good idea."

Leila rattled off her digits and Geneva entered them then pressed Call. Nothing.

She tried again. And again. Still no ring tone.

"Says it's out of service." Geneva held up her screen for Leila to see.

"Damn. I guess that's good at least. No one can run up my bill. Serves the crooks right for stealing it in the first place." Leila crossed her arms and sighed. "Tell me you're not going to stop at my brother's place on the way out of town. He doesn't deserve that courtesy, you know."

Geneva shrugged. "I was. Not to make amends or anything. Just to say thanks for letting me tour his facilities and interview his partners and clients. That's all."

"Like I said, more than he deserves, but you're a better person than me. I love Mark, don't get me wrong. Family is everything to us. But it's time he learned to hold himself to the same high standards he uses with everyone else."

"Right." Guilt stabbed Geneva in the heart again. Openness, honesty, truth. Those weren't such terrible things to ask from someone you wanted to have a relationship with, were they?

Her thoughts snagged.

Me? In a relationship with Mark?

Where she expected to have her usual recoil response from the commitment inherent in those words, Geneva found only peace this time. Peace and sorrow that she'd blown her chance at something more with Mark.

Oh, boy. Suddenly getting to the compound and seeing him seemed like the most important thing in the world.

"I need to get going." Geneva ran for the exit.

"Sure." Leila followed her to the door. "Tell Mark I'll stop by and check on him in the morning."

Geneva raced to the Brothers In Arms compound, her mind and heart reeling. What exactly should she say when she saw him? *Sorry I acted like a defensive bitch earlier, but I've got six toes on one foot. Sorry I'm a genetic freak, but would you like to be my boyfriend?*

Then again, she could always go with her favorite Jimmy Buffet line:

Let's get drunk and screw.

Ugh. For a woman who made her living from words, none of the right ones seemed to come. By the time she pulled into the compound parking lot, she was a jumble of nerves. Maybe Mark wouldn't even want to see her again. Maybe he hated her for not opening up to him.

Maybe...

She parked between Jace's used Range Rover and Mark's Jeep and got out. Mark's house across the way was dark, but lights were still on in the office, so she headed there first. Inside, she found Jace and Vann arguing.

"What the hell do you mean you fell asleep? You had one fucking job," Vann shouted.

"He was out cold on the couch," Jace said, his tone and movements agitated. "What else was I supposed to do, huh? And I said I'm sorry I dozed off. What more do you want me to say?"

"Um, hey," Geneva said tentatively from the doorway to announce her presence. "What's going on?"

"Mark's disappeared. That's what's going on." Vann shot Jace another glare. "We need to find him fast. He could be out there injured, alone, or worse."

"Right." Geneva's heart stumbled and her eyes widened. Bone deep fear for Mark shoved own insecurities aside. "His Jeep's still here."

"But the Humvee's gone," Vann said, giving her a flat look.

"Right." Geneva rubbed her arms. "Want me to call it in to the police?"

"Already did," Jace said. "First thing."

"Okay." She took a deep breath. She was a reporter. Finding things out was what she did for a living. *Get at it, girl.* "Where does he usually hang out? Besides here?"

"Leila's," Vann said and started for the door.

"Don't bother. I just came from there and he's not at Scoops." Geneva tapped the toe of her boot on the wooden floor, thinking. "Leila's phone was missing though."

"You think it's related?" Jace asked her.

"Could be." Geneva walked to Mark's desk and took a seat behind his computer. She taped a few keys to wake the screen. "Anyone know his password?"

"You're kidding, right?" Vann snorted. "We're in the security business, remember?"

"Right." Most systems gave you try strikes before locking up, so Geneva started typing in words she thought Mark might choose. She started with the most obvious. Leila.

Nope.

Tried something more intrinsic to who he was. Something Samoan. *Aiga.*

Nada.

Dammit.

She was about to ask the guys for suggestions when both of their cell phones buzzed simultaneously. Jace pulled his out first, frowning at the screen. "This message doesn't make any sense. Rig Man Win Cell?"

"Same here." Vann scrunched his nose, his gaze narrowed on Geneva. "Says it's from Leila's phone. But you said she lost it."

"She did. I tried calling it for her when I was at the café, but couldn't get a ring tone." Geneva moved in beside Vann and peered at his screen.

Rig Man Win Cell. Rig Man Win Cell.

The guys were right. It didn't make any sense. She closed her eyes and ran through all the time she'd spent with Mark—the first day in Scoops parking lot, scaling the bank building downtown, dinner afterward, the drive to the Rigsdale Mansion.

"Rig man. Do you think it has something to do with your rappelling class?"

"Nah." Jace wrinkled his nose. "Those were all Highway Patrol guys. Doubt any of them would want to kidnap Mark, no matter how rough he was on them."

"Win cell, win cell," Vann repeated over and over. "Some kind of contest?"

Geneva shook her head. "Too random. Hey, Jace. Mark always bragged about your mechanical skills. Think you can rig up one of these phones to give us more information about the coordinates this message came from?"

"I can try," he said, stalking to the corner with his own phone in hand.

"My guess is wherever Mark is, he doesn't have much time," Vann said, pacing the room again. "I can't help thinking this is tied to all the crazy shit happening lately. First the severed brake lines, then the Diesel Dome collapse…"

"The suicides that are murders. Oh, shit!" Realization dawned with sickening clarity. Geneva clutched Vann's arm. "What if the Rigsdales are involved with those too?"

"What?" Jace asked, facing them.

"How do you know about that?" Vann asked, his scowl dark.

Geneva took a step back. "Mark told me at the hospital. He said that he'd been investigating the suicides on his own, thinking they might not be suicides at all. What if he found out something incriminating about the Rigsdales? What if they sent some of their minions to do him in once and for all?"

Jace and Vann exchanged a look.

"Makes sense," Jace said. "Explains the first part of the message too."

"How?" Geneva frowned.

"Rig Man. Rigsdale Mansion."

"What about the second part?" Vann asked.

"We'll figure it out on the way." She grabbed Vann's phone from his hand and hit the redial button. The line clicked then went dead. "We need to get over to the mansion now."

Vann snatched his device back. "We need a plan first. They won't just let us in."

Geneva's nervous tension boiled over into irritation. Vann seemed to have taken an instant dislike to her. Fine. He wasn't the man she was interested in. But she sure as shit refused to let his personal issues with her get in the way of her saving the man she loved.

Loved?

Geneva swallowed hard.

Crazy as it sounded, yes, she had fallen head over heels for Mark Rogers and she sure as hell wasn't about to lose him now.

Determined, she marched back up to Vann and stood nose to nose. Well, more like nose to chest, given his height. "Then think fast, mister, because I refuse to stand around here while Mark could be beaten, tortured or killed. He told me about his theory on the suicides. Deal with it." Vann's stoic expression shifted slightly toward astonishment. "Yeah, that's right. Mark trusted me enough to share that with me today. So how about you lighten up and get over whatever the hell problem you seem to have with me, okay? We're all on the same side here. We all want Mark back safe and sound."

Jace chuckled. "Man, she told you."

Vann watched her closely, a muscle ticking near his tight jaw. "You've been spending too much time with Leila."

"And loving every minute of it," Geneva winked and stood her ground.

After exhaling slow, Vann gave a short nod. "Fine. How are we going to get him out?"

"We could try a bait and switch," Jace said, pulling out weapons from a gun cabinet across the room and handing them to Vann. "Like that time at the consulate in Kabul."

191

"Nah." Vann slammed a magazine into place in the butt of a semi-automatic, clicked on the safety, and sat it on the desk before grabbing a handgun from Jace. "Not enough time. Plus, we don't have a camel."

"Shit." Jace slid his arms into a torso holster then loaded up his Desert Eagles into the holster around his waist. "I guess we just blast our way in then. You want the cops to tag along or not?"

"Wait!" Geneva said, a new idea occurring. After all, it was the reason that had brought all of them together in the first place. Seemed fitting it would save them all in the end. "I think I have a way we can get in without any firepower at all. At least not of the ballistic kind."

"Really?" Vann frowned. "How?"

"The Rigsdales are all about PR, right? They love being in the public eye, flaunting their wealth and lifestyle. Let's give them what they want."

"An interview, you mean?" Jace said, his slow smile growing. "Fuck yeah!"

"More than a simple interview. A full-blown press conference. No way they won't come outside for that. Once the house is empty then you guys can get in and get Mark." Geneva grinned and fished out her phone from her bag. "All I have to do is call in a few favors."

CHAPTER TWENTY

"Good evening, this is Marcus Diego reporting live from the mansion of Tim and Kim Rigsdale in Ortega, California. I'm here tonight to interview journalist Geneva Rios about her startling new findings regarding the recent rash of Navy SEAL suicides here in California." Geneva smiled politely into the camera and said a silent prayer this would work. She'd wanted to be right about her hunches, she'd wanted a national headline and all that came with it, but she'd never, ever wanted any of it at the price of Mark's life.

"Tell us, Ms. Rios, how do you believe the Rigsdales are involved in these deaths?"

She froze, her mouth open, speechless.

Not good on national TV, but damn.

The guy behind the camera gestured wildly to her to keep talking. Geneva swallowed hard and did her best to pick up the topic of the piece again. "Well, Marcus, Tim and Kim Rigsdale are at the forefront of the Frank Sutton campaign for Congress and leaders of the controversial American Way Group, major donors to the Sutton campaign." Other journalists from competing media outlets crowded and jostled around her, all of them vying for the best spot to film. "Their views are decidedly racist, misogynistic, and xenophobic. By coming here tonight, I hope to draw them out and ask them face to face about the recent deaths of two ex-Navy SEALs. With the help of several sources, who wish to remain anonymous at this time, I've uncovered evidence that the suicides of these men may not have been suicides at all."

She glanced over to the side of the house and saw Jace and Vann disappear around a set of construction barricades. While she broke the news of their suspicions on national TV, they were going in search of Mark. With luck, they'd find him and spring him before anyone was the wiser and they could all escape unnoticed during the post-press conference melee.

Behind her, a murmur started through crowd and Geneva turned to see Kim Rigsdale emerge onto the front portico of the mansion. Flanked as she was by the tall white columns, she looked more like a wealthy southern socialite than the wife of some tech guru. As always, she was dressed to the nines, this time in a dark green designer dress and matching high heels, her makeup and hair done to perfection. She gave the gathered crowd a perfect, plastic smile. "My husband will be out shortly to address all of you. This visit is unexpected, but we always want to cooperate with our friends in the press."

The woman was a consummate liar. Geneva gave her that. She and her husband had to be shitting themselves right about now, considering they had a lawn full of uninvited, rabid reporters and a hostage somewhere in their house, but it seemed Kim Rigsdale had her Teflon public persona firmly in place.

After she glanced over at the construction area and still saw no sign of the guys or Mark, Geneva decided to try and buy them some more time. She pushed to the front of the crowd with her cameraman and stuck her recorder right into Kim's face.

"Ms. Rigsdale," Geneva asked. "We met the other day at the Sutton rally in Ortega. Geneva Rios with the National Tribune. Would you care to make a statement about the recent rash of suicides among Navy SEAL veterans?"

"Um…" Kim gave a nervous laugh and glanced around, as if looking for her husband. "Tim should be out in just a moment, He's far better equipped to answer your questions, Ms. Rios."

Taking her lead, several other reporters crammed into the space around Geneva and started bombarding Kim with questions as well. Good. If that bitch thought she could hurt the people Geneva cared for and get away with it, she was very much mistaken.

Soon, Tim emerged from the mansion, wearing a slick suit and a smile just as fake as his wife's, and moved beside Kim into the harsh media glare. He waved to the assembled press then stepped up to a podium that one of his beefy bodyguards carried out of the mansion and set up for him.

"Good evening, everyone," Tim said. "It's my understanding some disturbing allegations have been brought to light tonight, but I'm eager to set the record straight on why our candidate, Frank Sutton, is the absolute best choice for Congress and to answer any other questions you might have to the best of my abilities."

Like lions to a fresh kill, the reporters descended on the Rigsdales, everyone shouting questions over one another until there was nothing but a cacophony of confusion. Exactly what Geneva had hoped would happen. She stepped forward into the chaos to ensure the focus stayed on her and away from whatever might be happening with the guys and Mark.

"Mr. Rigsdale. Geneva Rios from the National Tribune again. Can you address the allegations of racism and sexism made against Frank Sutton and The American Way Foundation? What was your involvement in the SEAL suicides?"

Tim stared down at her, his expression neutral though his gaze sparked with anger. "Nice to see you again, Ms. Rios." His tone said the exact opposite. "I'd like to say here and now that neither we nor Mr. Sutton had any involvement in the tragic deaths of those SEALs and any slanderous rumors of biased behavior by The American Way Group are completely false. Mr. Sutton and all of us who believe in The American Way only want what's best for our country. We want to get America back to what it once was, back on top of the world, both economically and ethically."

"And who decides those ethics, Mr. Rigsdale?" Geneva countered. "You?"

Tim gave a derisive snort. "This country was built on certain values, Ms. Rios. Justice, truth, the pursuit of happiness for its rightful citizens. But perhaps those things are difficult to understand for an immigrant such as yourself."

Geneva bristled at his comment, but kept her composure. This pompous ass was digging his own grave deeper with every word out of his hateful mouth. Best of all, it was live on TV across the country. "I was born and raised in the USA, Mr. Rigsdale. Same as you. But thanks for asking." This got a snicker from the surrounding reporters. "And you really haven't answered my question."

"Well, I—" Tim's answer was interrupted by a loud clang issuing from somewhere near the west wing of the mansion. *Please don't let that be Mark and the guys. Please.* Tim signaled to his two bodyguards to go check it out, and then returned his attention to Geneva. "To answer your question, Ms. Rios. The prestigious members of The American Way Foundation include some of the most prominent businessmen and women in the world. They would never condone the exclusion of anyone based strictly on their race, religion or gender. We do, however, think society needs to rethink its values. We think—"

"No one cares what you think anymore, asshole," another man said. He shoved to the front of the crowd wearing a T-shirt for Sutton's opposition. "Why don't you just shut the hell up?"

Geneva's eyes widened. She'd not invited Sutton's opposition, but it appeared they'd turned up anyway. She wasn't sure how'd they'd heard about her impromptu press conference, but she was glad to add them to the distraction. The air sizzled with barely suppressed rage and she took the opportunity presented by the crowd's growing agitation to slip around the side of the stage and head for the front door of the mansion. Time was running out and eventually even a windbag like Tim Rigsdale would run out of excuses.

Once inside the house, she looked around trying to figure out which way to go. On the left, it looked like a home office. Toward the back was the kitchen and dining with stairs leading up to what she assumed were bedrooms. Turning her head to the right, she saw more construction. Taking a chance, she ran behind the tarp hanging over the doorway and down the hall. Every door she ran past was open and the rooms were filled with equipment or building materials. Reaching the other end of the mansion, she found an open door with steps leading down. Turning to see if she could hear anyone in the main part of the house, she took a chance and ran down the stairs.

199

Of course, wine cellar. Geneva kicked herself for not thinking of it sooner.

The wine cellar door was open. And empty. All that was left on the floor was the remnants of what looked like a smashed cell phone. Geneva picked it up and stared at the back. Engraved there were the words, "To Leila. My *aiga.*" She couldn't help but smile. Leave it to a SEAL to use what resources he had available.

There was a loud shout from outside and the sounds of a scuffle. Geneva tossed what was left of Leila's phone back on the ground then ran up the stairs and ducked out through a tarp-covered opening in the wall back into the yard. From what she could see, it looked like a bunch of protestors for Sutton's opposition were causing a ruckus with the Rigsdale supporters near the front of the house.

Perfect. Now if they could just get Mark out of there, they'd be all set.

An engine revved nearby and suddenly the space around her was flooded with halogen light. The Range Rover zoomed up beside her and Vann leaned out the window. "Hurry up and get in. Shit's hitting the fan down there and we need to get out of here."

Geneva didn't hesitate. She yanked open the back door on the driver's side and climbed in, relieved to see Mark slumped on the back seat beside her. He looked bruised and battered and more beautiful than anything she'd ever seen. Careful not to hurt his many wounds, she leaned over and carefully kissed him on the lips. "I'm glad you're okay."

"Me too," he said. "Sorry about the way things ended at the hospital. I was out of line—"

"No." Geneva put her fingers over his lips to silence him. "It was my fault."

"Hey, guys," Jace said, from the front passenger seat. "Can we save the moment until we get back to the compound? We still have to make it through that angry crowd."

Vann drove slowly forward, trying to avoid the mass of people yelling, screaming, and fighting each other. On the front portico, the two bodyguards Tim had sent after the guys had returned to his side, but appeared to be having a hard time keeping the crowds at bay. The Range Rover had almost reached the edge of the driveway when a gunshot cut through the noise surrounding them.

"What the fuck?" Jace shouted, pulling his own weapon.

"Get down!" Mark pushed Geneva toward the floor.

"Like hell!" She shrugged off his hold and peered out the window beside her. "Holy Shit! Tim Rigsdale is down! I think he's been shot! There's so much blood!"

The people at the rally went nuts, screaming, crying and running everywhere. Pandemonium ensued. Reporters hurried to the makeshift stage to get their money shots of the carnage and the last thing Geneva saw before her view was blocked by the crowds was Kim Rigsdale sinking to her knees beside her husband's body.

"Shit." Vann swerved hard to the left and out on to the driveway then accelerated fast. "We need to get off the estate before the cops arrive."

CHAPTER TWENTY-ONE

"I can't say how glad I am that you figured out my coded message," Mark confessed as he hugged Geneva against him. His body ached in places he didn't think possible but he would be damned if he would go to the hospital now. Not after everything that happened.

"Well, you can thank your brothers for that one," Geneva told him, smiling at the guys.

"The mansion part wasn't that hard but we were concerned once we got there. We knew we only had so much time with the distraction Geneva concocted." Vann seemed to look at Geneva with a newfound respect making Mark wonder what went on while he was held prisoner.

"We figured they'd want to keep you close but out of the way with everyone coming and going at the mansion. The abandoned construction was a bit like a giant neon sign pointing directly to you," Jace told him as he drank his beer. "I still can't believe the Rigsdales were behind the murders but there's no way to prove it. It's not like you managed to record anything."

Shaking his head, "No, what with the concussion and yet another accident, it didn't occur to me to carry any sort of recording device," Mark teased.

It was close to three in the morning by the time they all sat around the television in Mark's office. They'd grown silent as they stared at the television screen. The murder of Tim Rigsdale was breaking news on every station. Mark shook his head and sighed. "Guy spent his whole life trying to stay in the public eye and ends up dying to do it."

"Who shot him? That's what I'd like to know," Vann said. He pulled bottled water out of the mini-fridge against the wall and cracked it open. "From these news reports it sounds like they're trying to blame some crazed opposition supporter."

"You don't buy that?" Jace asked from his seat behind Mark's desk.

"Nah." Vann took a swig of water then pointed at the television screen. "See that replay. Whoever shot him used a laser sight. You can see a hint of the red dot just before the bullet was fired. That was a precise hit too. Only a trained marksman could've made it without harming anyone else or drawing attention to what they were doing."

"You're thinking military?" Jace frowned.

"Most likely." Vann glanced over at Mark, who sat on the sofa with Geneva beside him.

"Dammit!" At once, everyone turned to look at Jace who tossed his phone down. "That's another client who cancelled.

That article in the National Tribune really did a number on us. Between it and this damn assassination that's all over the news, we're going to have to fight to protect our reputation." Jace rubbed at his head in irritation.

"So who do we have coming in next?" Vann questioned.

Jace stood up and strode over to Mark's desk. Grabbing the file, he tossed it at Vann. "Some restaurant heiress. Mary Conde. She's all yours, man."

"*Mercy* Conde," Vann corrected him. His eyes scanned the file, flipping through the pages before returning to her photo. Mark caught his interested look but at this point, exhaustion was rapidly overtaking him and he still had some unfinished business.

"I think…" Mark took Geneva's hand then pushed to his feet. "That I'm tired of talking about this shit right now. I'll see you guys in the morning."

He didn't miss the look Jace gave him but Vann was too busy staring at the photo of their next client.

CHAPTER TWENTY-TWO

Mark led Geneva out into the cool evening then around the side of the building to give them a bit more privacy. "Listen. When I was locked up in that cellar, I had a lot of time to think." He kept a hold of her hand with his good one because it felt so awesome to touch her again. "I really am sorry about what I said back at the hospital, Geneva. Leila's always telling me I judge other people way harsher than I judge myself." He shook his head. "And she's right. I expected you to trust me, but wasn't willing to do the same for you. I'm sorry. If you want to keep your secrets, you can."

Geneva kicked a stone with the toe of her boot and gave a sad little chuckle. "Honestly, I really don't have any secrets from you anymore. I told them all." She scrunched her nose. "Well, except one."

"The boots?"

"The boots."

"Seriously, you can wear whatever shoes you want—"

"No. I want to tell you." She sighed then turned to face him. "I've got six toes."

"What?" Mark frowned. "Did you lose the other four?"

"No." Geneva shook her head. "I mean I've got six toes on one foot. That's why I wear these boots all the time. They're specially made with extra space for it." In the dim light from the nearby windows, he saw pink color suffuse her cheeks. "That's why I made you keep my socks on when we—"

"Because of an extra toe?"

"Yes." She threw up her hands in exasperation. "I'm a freak."

"Well yeah, but I don't think we can blame that all on your toe," he said, grinning.

"I'm serious." She gave him an annoyed look and crossed her arms. "My parents ended up homeschooling me because of it when I was younger. I got bullied all the time."

"Kids can be cruel." Mark took her hand again, pulling her away from the building and out into the parking lot, heading for his house. "But you can't live your life based on old fears. And I'm a freak too. Hell, we're all freaks. It's just some of us hide it better than others."

"Where are we going?" she asked, once they reached his front porch.

"I want to show you something inside." Mark fished his keys out of his pocket with his right hand then unlocked the door. "C'mon."

"I've heard that line before, buddy." Geneva snorted. "You just want to get laid."

"That too." Mark pulled her inside, and then slammed the door behind them before picking her up in his arms. His body ached and his ribs were killing him, but right now all he could imagine was lying in his bed with this beautiful woman and making her scream his name in ecstasy.

"Be careful!" Geneva scolded, twining her hands around his neck. "You'll hurt yourself again."

"I'm fine." Mark took the stairs two at a time despite his injuries and her added weight, and didn't stop until he'd tossed her into the center of his king-sized bed. "Or I will be, once you're naked."

She giggled as he pulled off her boots, disrobed her, then himself, leaving them both nude, except for one thing.

Slowly, Mark kissed his way down Geneva's gorgeous body, taking extra time to worship her lovely breasts and belly, before working his way down her thighs and calves to her stockinged feet. Keeping his gaze locked with hers, he slowly tugged off her right sock. She tensed. "Okay?"

Geneva exhaled slowly then nodded. "Okay."

Once her toes came into view, all six of them, his heart swelled with affection. How could anything so cute ever be considered freaky? He bent and kissed each one, lavishing them with the attention they deserved before removing her left sock and proceeding to do the same.

By the time he was done, Geneva had relaxed back into the bed and was smiling serenely. He kissed his way up her body to nuzzle her ear. "I adore every square inch of you, Geneva Rios. And having that extra toe just means there are more of you to love."

She pulled him down for a heated kiss. "Are you sure?"

"Positive." He cupped her breast gently and stroked her nipple. "Like I said, I had a lot of time to think in that cellar. About what's important. About whom I want in my life."

Geneva met his eyes, tears gathering in hers. "Me?"

"You."

"Flaws and all?" she asked, her voice still a tad hesitant.

"Flaws and all." Mark slid his right hand down her belly to ease her thighs open and smiled. "Especially, the all."

"Oh, Mark. I've done a lot of thinking too and I don't know how to say this…that is to say…I think. No, I know. I…."

Mark stilled as Geneva tried to speak. He felt as though he'd been kicked all over again. Was she about to tell him she didn't want to be with him? After everything? He wasn't sure he wanted to hear what she had to say. Not now. Not after, he'd opened up to her.

He grunted, as he levered up one arm, his ribs screaming at him to stop. "Look Geneva. You don't want…."

"Stop."

"No, let me say this, I get that…." He stopped talking as he watched Geneva scoot slowly down the bed, her body brushing enticingly against him, as she worked her way down. If this was some sort of tease on her part, he was not in the mood. Narrowing his eyes at her, he was about to say something when she lightly placed her finger over his lips before kissing him.

"What I was attempting to say is, "I love you, Mark Rogers. I don't know when or how, but in such a short amount of time, I've fallen in love with you." Geneva punctuated her words with kisses on his face before shifting to his neck. "And if you would stop being so obstinate and let me actually get the words out, I would happily say it again."

A slow smiled spread across Mark's face, as Geneva nibbled on his ear. When she didn't say anything else, he cleared his throat making her look up at him.

"What?"

Shifting to his back, he dragged Geneva on top of him as he grinned at her. "This is me, not being obstinate. So, say it again. Please."

Her chuckle made his balls tighten painfully while her hair tickled his chest. Shifting to her knees, she leaned over him, kissing him deeply. When they parted, they were both panting.

"I, Geneva Rios, love you, Mark Aleki Rogers. Flaws and all."

Reaching for her, Mark pushed her over and rolled quickly so he was on top of her. He caught his breath while he forced the pain down. Looking down at her, he kissed her. "And I, Mark Aleki Rogers, love you, Geneva Rios. Flaws and all. But can we please save the acrobats for tomorrow. I'd really like not to have to go to the hospital again."

Her answering chuckle was music to his ears.

END OF SEAL DEFENDER

Brothers In Arms

Book One

PLUS: Do you like your heroes *strong, powerful* and in *uniform*? Read an exclusive excerpt from Leslie North's bestselling novel "Shooting the SEAL".

THANK YOU!

Thank you so much for purchasing and reading my book. It's hard for me to put into words how much I appreciate my readers. If you enjoyed this book, please remember to leave a review. I want to keep you guys happy! I love hearing from you :)

For all books by Leslie North visit:

Her Website: LeslieNorthBooks.com

Facebook: www.facebook.com/leslienorthbooks

Get SIX full-length, highly-rated Leslie North Novellas FREE! Over 548 pages of best-selling romance with a combined 634 FIVE STAR REVIEWS!

Sign-up to her mailing list and get your FREE books:

Leslienorthbooks.com/sign-up-for-free-books

Sneak Peek

Shooting the SEAL
Saving the SEALs Book One

Blurb

With the clock ticking, Navy SEAL Gage Jackelsn must uncover the truth about his fallen teammate before he and his brothers-in-arms take the blame. When his intel leads him to a publishing company, he never dreamed he'd end up as a romance cover model. He'll do whatever it takes to get closer to the information he needs, but when he meets Anna—the photographer with the striking eyes and sultry voice—it just may be worth it.

Photographer Anna Middleton has shot her share of male models, but none that are real-life SEALs. She's not sure why the tall, muscular military man would want to pose as a romance hero, but she doesn't have much time to wonder before her boss disappears under suspicious circumstances. Soon she's thrust into the middle of a situation that could mean life or death.

When Gage realizes how much trouble Anna is in, he'll do what he can to shield her from the danger that always follows him. But with the scars from her past that she keeps hidden, can Anna ever trust him if she learns their meeting was based on a lie?

Get your copy of Shooting the SEAL from:

<u>www.LeslieNorthBooks.com</u>

Shooting the SEAL
Saving the SEALs Book One

Excerpt

Gage Jackelson decided he'd rather be in the middle of a fire fight on open water than standing in the front of a green screen in nothing more than his jeans, feeling like a hunk of meat on a slab.

What looked like a Gothic fairy—heavy on the black eyeliner and dyed hair and complete with what looked a pink tutu trimmed in more black—flitted about him, dusting powder on him and muttering about cheekbones.

This was ridiculous. He stood, arms folded, wondering how he could get out of this. But he couldn't. He had to start thinking of this like a mission. So he let the fairy fuss.

The elevator pinged, and he hoped the photographer had finally arrived and he could wrap up this charade, get the intel they needed, and get his shirt back on. The things he'd do for a friend—even a dead one.

Hearing steps, he glanced over and watched a young woman walk into the studio—okay, warehouse was a better name for it. A loft with more ceiling space than floor space, white walls and photos hung on them. Dirt glazed the windows, but he had enough light on him that he kept breaking a light sweat.

The woman stepped in front of him, head cocked, and stared at him. He could feel his skin warm. He'd been on the other side of that kind of assessment—had been eyeing the girls just last week with Scotty making his usual crude remarks, and Spencer sipping his tequila. This woman would have rated a second look and one of Scotty's terrible pick-up lines.

Eyes blue as the Mediterranean Sea fixed on him. Tight jeans encased long legs—he'd always been a leg man—and a white silk blouse said she had money enough to afford good clothes. Golden hair had been pulled back from a heart-shaped face. She didn't wear much makeup that he could see, and he caught a flash of gold earrings. But those eyes kept pulling him back for another look. Who the hell was she? The photographer's girlfriend?

Turning, she walked over to the camera—not a digital, but something big and old and also expensive-looking. She stared through the lens and then looked up at him. "Gage Jackelson," she said the name as if she was thinking of something else. She propped a fist on one hip. "I keep wondering why'd a Navy SEAL agree to a cover shoot." A guy could feel quite warm wrapped up in her sultry tone.

He lifted an eyebrow. "And you are?"

She stepped up and reached out to shake his hand. "Anna Middleton."

Gage nodded. The photos on the walls all had Middleton signed to them. He was going to guess not the photographer's wife—no ring on her finger. He fought the urge to hold her hand longer than he should, but he caught a flush of color in her cheeks. She tilted her head up to look at him and he could swear he caught a flash of surprise in those sea-blue eyes.

Pulling her hand back, he watched as she tucked it behind her back before turning to grab the camera off its stand.

"Did Linda explain how this works?"

Linda—the Gothic fairy—flashed a smile at him. She trailed a finger down his forearm. "You'll do great. He's set, Anna." She ducked away.

Gage glanced at Anna and her camera. "How hard is it to smile for the camera?" Gage drawled. His fingers stopped tingling since he touched her, and he was itching to do so again. Or possibly run his fingers through that soft cloud of hair.

"You'd be surprised." Her wide mouth twitched at the corners. "We'll start without props, but Linda will bring a few in later."

"Props?" Gage lifted both eyebrows.

Anna took a couple of shots, the camera clicking. "We use a green screen so we can drop in any background, but it's easier to use anything that you will be touching in the actual photos." Stepping back to the tripod, Anna set the camera on it. She looked through the camera lens, paused and looked back up at him. "Um, you're looking a little stiff."

Linda gave a snort of amusement, tried to hide it with a cough. Gage smiled, and Anna gave Linda a dirty look before turning back to Gage. "Any chance you can relax? Loosen up? Look less like you're standing in front of a camera?"

Gage forced a smile. He was going to kill Scotty and Spencer for talking him into being the one to come to Coran Williams Publishing. *This is for Nick*, he told himself again. And they had damn little to go on right now—an encrypted flash drive and one personal photo that had been of Nick and Natalie. They hadn't even found Nick's awards and honors for service. But the photo had led them here.

"Mr. Jackelson?"

Gage shook himself out of his mood—he'd been starting to frown. He had to watch that. They'd talked it over and all had agreed that busting in here with questions might not get them far. They needed intel, meaning they needed to get inside this place and poke around. Which was why he was here. With his shirt off.

Get your copy of Shooting the SEAL from:

www.LeslieNorthBooks.com

43373101R00128

Made in the USA
Middletown, DE
07 May 2017